ISBN 978-1-7331185-1-4

Wilderness House Press
145 Foster Street
Littleton MA 01460

www.wildernesshousepress.com

Wilderness House Literary Review
www.whlreview.com

Book designed by Steve Glines
Text: Gandhi Serif

Cover painting *Red, Blue, Green* by Digby Beaumont
Author Photo by A. J. Savastinuk

OFFICE

A Novel

Susan Isla Tepper

Wilderness House Press

for Simon Perchik
who listened via phone
chapter by chapter
day after day
with his great humor and wisdom

Acknowledgments

FIRST AND FOREMOST, to my dear husband, Miles Tepper, straight from my heart for his patient kindness and understanding during these three uncertain tumultuous years. When our life turned upside down and inside out. Without him, I could never have written this book from the perspective of satire and dark humor.

I also wish to effusively thank everyone who read the manuscript and gave me such terrific blurbs, despite all they had going on with their own lives: Alexis Rhone Fancher, Harvey Araton, DeWitt Henry, Anne Elezabeth Pluto, Ron D'Alena, and Doug Holder. I am so grateful for your time and your friendship.

To my dear friend, Digby Beaumont, who has also been my collaborator on many poetry / prose / artwork projects, I thank you so very much for the gracious loan of your unique painting that perfectly represents the book and serves it well as its dynamic cover.

For my brother, Christopher Bruno, who I haven't seen in nearly three years but who is a great cheerleader of my writing (plus the true owner of the #21 jersey) I thank you for listening to my endless commentary about the book each week over the phone. Despite that your dog Bandit was terribly jealous, making jealous dog noises and demands, 'cause you weren't paying attention to him!

And, last, but not least, I wish to thank my long-time friend and editor Steve Glines for publishing another book of mine. This one!

A Special Thanks to Chad Parenteau and Jason Wright
who published the first two chapters
at Oddball Magazine
in a slightly different form

OFFICE

He was lost and he was set free.
— Graham Greene, A CHANCE FOR MR LEVER, 1936

PART ONE

CHAPTER 1

The Employee – The Light and The Dark

It's mid-month and the office is down in the doldrums. Or, should I say what is left of the office. Most split after the first covid wave. A few here, a few there. Quinn called it *leaving in drips and drabs*. This huge space is now an empty monument to commerce. Three girls who hung in through the various variants finally left last month. *Working from home makes them feel safer* was the party line. All three have long black hair, pillow lips and perfect manicures. And too many aliases on too many dating sites. Plus, nobody was doing any work; they just hung out collecting a paycheck. Frankly I was glad to see them go. Especially Tanya. That one looked dangerous. Quinn said they were *on the dole*. An older guy from Ireland who grew up seeing it all, or at least hearing about the bad ole days— he tells me the office occupancy rate here in midtown is only at roughly 30 per cent.

"We should buy some space and turn it into Air BNB," he says.

"This is New York City. Buildings are designated for certain usage," I tell him. "You can't just plunk a mattress down and sell tourists a place to sleep."

Quinn doesn't look deterred.

⁕

Later, after coming back from his favorite lunch joint— one of the Irish bars on 6ᵗʰ with the hot plate buffet that lets you in without a vaccine card— when I popped my head over the plexiglass barrier I saw him checking out BNB on his computer.

"It's a crazy idea," I tell him.

"Here's what's crazy," Quinn says. "The babes are home while we're here. The night janitor is here. And a few of those interns looking to ladder-hop while everyone is huddling from the plague. I plan on making hay."

Meaning money. Everywhere Quinn looks he sees potential. It's why my country was able to pull up and out he's fond of saying. He mentions it again. I say nothing back because I don't want to hear about the potato famine, horrible as it was with people eating bugs and nettles to stay alive. Not that I'm unsympathetic. I worked my way through college. I do know a certain hardship kind of life. Quinn also frequently speaks of his love for America. I definitely don't get involved on that score. When people start to love this country, or their mother country, is their choice. At least I'm fairly confident he won't come in here some day with a high powered rifle.

"We need to spruce up this place," I say. Hoping to turn his attention away from the BNB business.

"OK. I'll bring some Christmas bling tomorrow. We'll put a shine on this office."

✣

When I arrive at 9, a gigantic *Merry XMAS!* wreath is covering the entire white board; which nobody writes on anymore; since there are no meetings or tactics to discuss. Maneuvering around it, I almost crash into a card table draped in green felt. Also set too close to the door. This office is humungous. You could stage a bullfight. Why jam everything together?

"You approve?" Quinn seems to twinkle all over.

On the card table is the biggest crystal punch bowl I've ever... with at least a dozen matching crystal cups attached by little crystal S hooks.

For the first time I notice points on his ear tops, like devil ears. "I'm going to brew up the best punch you'll ever pour down your gullet," he's saying. Quinn's pleasure full to overflowing.

Staring at his ears I'm wondering whether smoke will rise from the punch bowl. Life has become a strange potpourri. "Do those little cup hooks come off or they're stationary?"

"They come off. Nothing in this world is stationary, Mate, or didn't you notice? Why hang thirty hooks when you might only have ten guests?"

He has a point. But the table is still in a bad spot. "Does this have to be so close to the door? People are going to bump into it. The mailman, for instance. I almost knocked it myself coming in just now."

"Okey doke. Take an end and we'll slide it a bit."

"Has the Boss approved this party?"

"The wife is in crisis mode, again. He's not coming in."

We each take an end moving the card table.

"Better?" he says.

"Yeah."

I bend to pitch-roll a dime where the floor slopes but not so much that you'd notice. Pitch-roll got started when the place began to empty out. When our heads felt like empty drums like this punch bowl with nothing to do but sit there. My dime doesn't go far, I must've missed the sweet spot.

"I should've laid down a twenty," Quinn says rubbing his hands together.

"Shoulda coulda woulda," I say.

"Huh?"

"Is betting legal in your country?"

"Why'd you ask?"

"I don't know," I say shrugging a shoulder.

"One shoulder that's kind of girlie," he says.

A payback about the betting? Does he have a gambling problem? I decide it's best to let it go. I know who I am. "Nobody pitches like the Boss," I say.

Quinn's fuddling with his punch bowl. "I invited the girls," he says. "For Christmas cheer. This afternoon."

"Tanya?"

"Mate, she is one of *the girls*."

Meaning the three regulars. Not the job hoppers who shoot in and out of here. If this pandemic ever ends Tanya will be back, I suppose. Life is a trade-off.

"What are you planning on putting in your punch bowl?"

"A secret recipe from my Mam from back home. Can't tell you or she'll come down and haunt me from heaven."

"She must have been a good person to land in heaven."

Quinn scratches his stubbly chin. "That's a point of debate."

"What time is this big bash?"

"Three o'clock." He's nodding his head. "This way we have the light and the dark."

It seems important that his party should take place during daylight and nighttime. I don't get the significance.

Later, when he invites me to join him at the pub for lunch, I hold up my ham sandwich wrapped in Saran. "Have a nice lunch," I say. Thinking *Have a safe lunch*.

⚜

At 3 p.m., more or less, the girls wander in, ditching their coats wherever. They carry on over the punch bowl as if it were an asteroid fallen to earth. Like they never saw a punch bowl in their lifetime? Quinn is bowing and preening, stressing it's Waterford Crystal and would cost thousands if bought here in New York City.

Tanya says, "You mean to say you carted that punch bowl and all the little cups here from Ireland?"

"And the crystal ladle," I say. "You can't have a punch bowl without a good ladle."

Quinn is so proud he's rocking. "You should see all the Waterford the family had shipped over."

"It must have cost a fortune if they charged by weight," I say.

Dipping the ladle into rose colored punch he continues smiling, filling a cup two-thirds. "Here you go, Allie." She dimples and makes a little curtsy.

She's tallest of the three. I feel a curtsy would suit a shorter girl better. Not that curtsies are the norm these days. Women are more likely to kick you in the balls.

Allie sips the punch and makes a thumbs up. "Delish!"

This is the first time I've ever seen all three of them standing together. They look like a sister act. All that black hair, and Tanya and Stella being almost the same height. You could put Allie in the middle with the others flanking her. Give them a mic and they could sing *Rockin' Around The Christmas Tree*. It dawns on me that this has no relevance. If I mention it, it would somehow put a damper on Quinn's gathering. They wouldn't find it humorous. It would piss them all off. What's the difference how tall we are? they'd say with varying degrees of aggression. Everyone stiffening around the punch bowl. The jovial mood broken. Actually, they do seem in much better spirits now that they don't have to come in to work. The new consultant, DeGrande, takes the ladle from Quinn. "I'll play bartender," he says, "you enjoy yourself a while."

They all seem to love the whole punch bowl thing. I am pretty much being ignored.

By around five everyone is sloshed. The darkness has taken over and given the office a whole different mood. Each of the three girls takes a turn sitting on Quinn's lap. Even a few interns get in on the fun. Nobody has asked to sit on my lap. The beat-up old janitor comes by to empty the trash bins. DeGrande hands him a cup.

"Good grog," says the janitor. The laughing girls gather 'round him their cheeks bright. Already tipsy, he holds out his cup for another fill. His mop handle bangs hitting the floor. Everyone laughs.

I slip out the door, unnoticed.

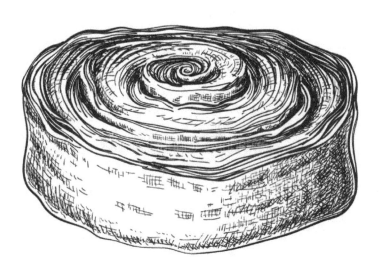

CHAPTER 2

The Boss – Grooming

As Boss, I make the decisions here. I don't approve or disapprove when the girls decide to set up a grooming station at the rear of the office near the women's bathroom. The point is to give women a big lift after staying home from work during the lockdown. A new hairdo, or nail treatment. I totally get that. All within walking distance or a quick elevator ride from their own office suite in this building. Tanya's brain child. *No Need To Leave To Be Lovely Again* reads her professionally made sign; scotch-taped to the glass window of a shut down lobby store that's been Rosie's Coffee Hub long as I've worked here. The cockroaches in there you had to step around— roaming freely for crumbs. I always took my coffee and iced Danish to go. One time I saw an old Chinese guy, suit and tie, pick one off the wall, crushing it in his fingers. My year in Iraq I saw bugs and more bugs. But that day at Rosie's really took the polish off my Danish.

Apparently Mario and the other two doormen are going along with Tanya's beauty scheme. They run a tight ship. It's their lobby. If someone drops dead down there, or pulls a knife, whatever, they're the ones the lawyers pounce on for interrogatories, depositions, court; etc etc etc. Tanya must've concocted some inappropriate promise to Mario that she plans not to keep. I've been in that same position, myself (ahem) with Tanya.

At any rate, the main room of our office suite is an extremely long space. I never walked it actually clocking the precise, though it's easily 30 times longer than wider. And there's no real work here, now, per se; so this beauty parlor thing is not in anyone's way. So far. Whether the corporation will keep going at this rate is the big looming question mark. Speaking of which— in-between four chairs the girls have managed to hang thick plastic sheeting from the ceiling. How they got it tacked up there is anyone's guess. At least they're trying to make it safe for their beauty customers. I don't know what amount of walk-in traffic they expect. This building now less than half occupied.

✤

The other day I cut through Grand Central during lunch time and it was *The Twilight Zone*. A mere scattering of people. The usual crush was a distant dream. I stopped to stare at the big clock. Then I got this weird craving for The Oyster Bar. I haven't thought about going there for more than a decade; or three. Stepping in with a blonde on my arm. The soaring ceiling coved and glittering above the simple red and white checkered table cloths. *Casual chic* they call it. Noisy. Those gleaming oysters shucked and spread across an ice bed with lemon wedges and cups of red sauce tucked in. Before smart phones, a big square landline was brought to your table by a server in starched white, like a doctor, who plugged it into the wall announcing: *For you, Sir.* People noticed and could be seen murmuring: Who is *that*? I said it myself, on occasion.

Past three decades since I slurped those oysters! Christ! Now I've got a pounding headache. *Tempus fugit.*

I shout in to Tanya behind the plastic but she hasn't got aspirin. So far this morning the girls have one customer. A dame they call Marge with big eye bags and a tight head of short, orange curls.

Kenny strolls over. "That one in there is past the point of no return."

"You got any aspirin?"

He flexes. "Sorry, Boss." A smug type with that Ivy League face and spiked hair. Interesting contrast. I can't really challenge his wisecrack because women today don't look anything like that Marge. Another Twilight Zone moment.

We stand there staring at the plastic. "Tanya's the ringleader," I say. God knows what transformation she's promised this woman. The other two, Stella and Allie—they just go along. Not a lot of brain power, all in all.

Kenny moves toward the Poland Spring cooler. "Boss you want water?"

Now why the hell would I want water when I don't have aspirin? I notice the bottle is getting low. Mental note: contact the vendor. Rae, my secretary, would normally take care of it but she left some time ago. Kenny comes back carrying a single cup.

"We need more damn business. Drum it up," I tell him. "We've got to keep them too busy for this beauty parlor crap."

"Drum up business? Boss, you want me to stand on the street

playing guitar like the naked cowboy?" He laughs, drinks his water then twirls the empty cup on his fingertip.

"Is that guy still out there strumming?"

"It's winter, Boss, I doubt it."

"I'm not so sure." We take our time moving toward the front of the room. All these empty cubicles. How long can I go on justifying the cost?

This is a fucked up city. From the naked painted ladies taking pictures with tourists in Times Square, a few summers back, to the naked guitar guy. Topless women protesting something or other in Washington Square Park. Why all this flesh trade? I first spotted the naked cowboy out on that narrow center island, cars whizzing by him in both directions, playing his guitar with his long hair blowing, where the street loops on the east side of midtown to circle back around the pocket park.

"How do you think the guitar guy gets paid?" I say. "Who is behind that stunt?"

Kenny whistles looking around. "Panhandles. People shove bills in his guitar. And, other places." He hoots. Knows more than he lets on. His uncle was a mob boss shot to death in his own car during a sweep. Kenny's mother saw it all play out on crime TV.

"In the end women are behind everything," Kenny says like reading my mind.

A sudden loud screech pierces the space. We both turn looking back toward the plastic. "What the hell now?" I say.

"Tanya maybe gave the old broad a bikini wax." Kenny grabs his crotch. "Ouch!"

"Christ!" We could get cited; or something. I don't know the rules for this sort of practice. "Don't you have to be licensed by the state?" I say.

He blubbers up laughing. "Boss, you're one smart guy," he finally says sobering up. "But rules and regulations – out the window. Anything goes. Nobody's working in those departments now. You can put up a skyscraper and they won't even come snooping for a building permit."

DeGrande, the new consultant, has this annoying habit of appearing from behind. He just did it again. The guy bugs me. I can't put my finger on it. What the hell made me hire him? I must be losing my grip. Too much happening on every score.

Wild laughter erupts behind the plastic and we turn and look again.

Why? Are we expecting a mirage? Perhaps the woman has

been transformed into another type of red head. I've been married a long time. I jiggle change in my pocket. A young Ann-Margret type would work OK for me.

"I guess the old broad is sleek and ready," says Kenny.

He peels a piece of gum. We continue watching the plastic. It doesn't move. Nobody pushes through to walk out in splendor. Nobody parts the waters.

CHAPTER 3

The Boss – New Consultant

For a new hire, DeGrande has too many opinions coming too fast. In my opinion. I'm wondering again why I hired him. I start poking holes in one of his opinions to see what he's made of, when Lewis steps in saying, "We're open to all ideas. And glad to have you onboard as consultant. Isn't that so?"

What the...? raising my eyebrows. Did Lewis tell him to apply here? Maybe they're in cahoots.

"Isn't that so, Boss?" Lewis is challenging me. Thinks it will show-off his initiative. He should know. In better times I'd have canned his ass by the end of the day. I just clap him on the back and smile.

I'm the Boss, and that means secretly, or not so, they all hate you. Period. Even though you're a small boss in a shrinking market. Very. Like a wool sweater washed in hot water (sorry, we hit the wrong temperature button). So shrunken it has become impossible. Sometimes you forget why. Why you continue to come here. But, you, too, have bosses to answer to. And report to. And, so on and so forth.

"Roger. Or, right on," I tell Lewis, as if to seal the deal. He's happy and DeGrande is happy. What-the-fuck-ever.

These days you never know what is considered appropriate. Especially with the women. I heard a delivery guy call Tanya *Miss*. I halted in my tracks waiting for the squall. She was surprisingly lenient that day. The day of the widescreen. Ordered by her for the office and billed to the company.

"You had no authority," I told her after it was set up.

Ignoring this she said, "Please tip Lang." He must be the store guy hanging around.

"Why should the company..."

"Take it out of petty cash?" She gave me a coy smile.

Rolling a toothpick side to side in his mouth, Lang watched this all play out.

Petty cash! Who the hell keeps a petty cash drawer the last 40 years?

When I stood my ground Tanya said, "Well from wherever you get the liquor money."

I feigned ignorance. Liquor purchases? Tanya stood *her ground* with a hard stare aimed my way. I took out a twenty and handed it to the set-up guy. Lang. He barely acknowledged.

※

This is the world we live in. When it's slow around here (every day) they camp out in 6 foot chair spreads watching the widescreen. To show my general disapproval I don't join in which is just as well. Today, when I walk past, they're glued to a medi-fomercial involving an infected belly button. The narrator, a doctor or actor-doctor, is saying *Most* (but not all) *navel infections are the result of a botched navel ring procedure.*

"Home job. A do-it-yourself," says DeGrande. More words of wisdom from our new consultant. Though I still haven't heard anything innovative out of him on product.

"Where else would you do it?" says one of the girls. I forget her name. Sandra? Cassandra?

They look toward our new consultant. DeGrande stands. He spreads his hands palms up. "Where would you do it? At a sterile facility licensed and equipped to pierce anywhere on the body that suits your fancy."

Howling laughter breaks out. I have to suppress a laugh myself. Tanya trots over to the reception area, those high heels clicking on the faux marble. We've been minus a receptionist more than a year. Digging around underneath that area, she straightens up shaking a bag over her head. "Cheetos! Cha Cha Cha!"

One of the girls shrieks. "No way Cheetos! No way! They look like the belly button worms!"

Sandra? Cassandra? Which one is making the big ruckus? Humping her chair backward, while in it, the girl distances herself from the screen.

I pause to take a look.

It is pretty disgusting up close. Someone yells *Cheetos* again like a war cry. Tanya passing the Cheeto bag around. The girl who shrieked begins shrieking all over again. God almighty. Can't she just say no!

This particular Cheeto, blown up across the widescreen, happens to be flesh colored: like a bent worm emerging out of the belly button skin folds. Babies still attached to the mother crosses my mind. I picture my wife, Janice. Desperate for a kid.

The medi-fomercial has moved on to even more disgusting

examples of longer, fatter, twisted skin worms. The worst cases have yellowish-brown pus and other goop in the mix. The worse the worms, the more the hysterical shrieking. I can't shake that umbilical cord image.

Of course women see the whole thing differently, as a kind of reverential end to the delivery. I had an aunt who saved all three of her kids umbilical cords in pickle jars; preserved by some type of fluid. Tommy, my cousin, showed me his jar when we were both in the eighth grade. She'd labelled each with a kid's name printed on white antiseptic tape. No quibbling over whose was whose. Would it matter?

Then DeGrande calls out, "What's that green one circling the drain?" and they all screech with laughter collapsing in the chairs.

"Well," I say, "I'm sure glad we got our money's worth on the widescreen." And make my way toward my office in the rear of this ridiculously long empty room.

✢

Nowadays. A sigh that's more of a long groan pops out. Nowadays the dimensions of this place irk me. A hollow cavern. Used to hold dozens upon dozens of office workers. The space could be put to better use— for just about anything — an indoor soccer stadium for kids. Of course I exaggerate; to keep from blowing my brains out.

Kenny is calling out to me but I ignore him.

Midway back there, for no particular reason, I stop walking; taking in the bland painted walls. Tan. A person could go insane surrounded continually by tan. When the cubicles were filled and everyone put up their photos, cards, mementos, Valentine memoirs and plants and stuffed animals— the perimeter walls went unnoticed. A cheery buzz rose from those cubicles. People working yet surrounded by things they love. There's mileage in that. Someone hung a dog collar and chain that belonged to their deceased beagle. People would touch those items and ask about the dog, then pet pictures were exchanged, tears welling from untimely canine and feline departures. Is death ever timely?

Thank god I've never had to market a tan product. It would be brutal. Product marketing. You start to think about everything you see in that light. Brain-washing being closer to the truth. What truth? Mine is mine and yours is yours. But the real trick here is in the envelope: Push it way past its glue date.

CHAPTER 4

The Boss – Ear Swabs

In my less than spacious office I sit in my swivel chair. Black leather. Black— a power color. Black is *the buck stops here.*

You'd think in this huge space they could've spared a few more feet for the two puny offices boxed in down at the end here. The desk made from some walnut type wood or similar. I keep the desk top empty but for my laptop and a couple of pens, and a framed photo of Justine in a rowboat on Schroon Lake. I pick up the picture, study the small white boat, silvery water peaking from the breeze, Justine. Shot from the shore just before I waded in. It was meant to be a cheer-up weekend after the last miscarriage. I'd lied to her. Saying the picture was far too beautiful not to be framed in sterling silver. The truth— the goddamn truth— that day of the picture Justine looked pale and peaky.

DeGrande is tapping on my glass door but I wave him away. Feeling a big slump come over me.

How much longer? This baby factory Justine's got going. Our third program in our third hospital. She's turned 43. The baby doc hinting that we're reaching the finishing line. *Adopt* he said. Justine went ballistic. "Honey," I said to her, "how much can a couple endure?" She went ballistic on me, then.

I move the pens and Justine's picture off the desk onto the top of a metal file cabinet. Who files anymore? Shoving the laptop into an empty file drawer. The make-a-baby procedures. Not covered by insurance. She should have started back in her early thirties. Women want things both ways but nature has its own agenda. I don't dare tell Justine she waited too long. If some miracle occurs in the next few weeks that results in an actual birth, I'll be near to 70 when the kid goes to college. Retirement is a pipe dream.

From the bottom drawer of the desk I take out a can of Lemon Pledge squirting the desktop. Brings back a million memories. My mom used Lemon Pledge on all the wood in the house. This desk is covered in white dust and looks gummy. From the roll of paper towels the janitor left in my coat closet, I tear off the wrapping, wiping the desk down till it gleams a dark fresh sheen. The cleaning staff are supposed to take care of all this. According to the latest text they've been reduced down to one janitor per floor. Learn to live in filth, I'm thinking. I inhale the lemon scent deeply thinking some things never change. Until my dad caught me out, I used to squirt the wood furniture then finger paint the wet. That childish game enraged him. Twenty lashes and grounded for a couple weeks. I don't believe in corporal punishment. Certainly not for children.

When the desk looks dry and clean I put back Justine's picture. That adoption advice— sent her into a very dark place. If I told her once I told her fifty times: *You're getting the baby room ready too early.* But, nope... This last go 'round she was so sure.

Leaning the chair back, I put my feet up crossed at the ankles. No question the thick soled sneakers will mar the fresh wood sheen. *Luster* it says on the can. Luster is a beautiful word. Brings up visions of ravishing brunettes under chandeliers in long white sparkling gowns.

Justine wants her baby— like those people in the far northern climes who want the sun to come out.

DeGrande— dammit! has returned; rap-tap-taping again. I motion him in then listen to his spiel without paying attention. "Good job," I say. "That should work out well." Declining his invitation to lunch with some bullshit about a private call coming in.

CHAPTER 5

The Boss – Protests

This job— at least gets me out of the apartment 9 to 5 (ish). By the time I make a stop for a beer, pick up the dry cleaning or get a few items we don't need from the market, sometimes stopping at the flower stand for a fifteen dollar bouquet— walking home the rest of the way it's pushing on seven p.m.

The streets of New York empty by comparison. My thoughts have become a study in comparisons. The boredom of all this— indescribable. One dog walker handling a pack of happy unruly mutts can lift my spirits for blocks. You don't know what you miss until it's gone (they paved paradise...). Ah, Joni. Now there was a set of pipes.

I stare unseeing through the glass door that separates me from the long room of empty cubicles. I suppose I should call a work moratorium. Send the few still left here packing. They'll find jobs, firms are begging. When things actually do pick up, again, in this decade or the next, I'll have no staff. Everyone will be at home, working elsewhere, or dead. The irony of it. Almost makes me chuckle.

The other day I gave Kenny and Lewis the morale boost pitch: *There is only so much product marketing you can dredge up in a lagging economy. Most of our clients pulled when TV ad prices went through the roof. Now basically all you've got are car ads, insurance companies and pharma. Pharma fleshes out the commercials for the slip and fall lawyers.*

"I guess things could be worse," Kenny said when I paused.

For emphasis I added, "Notice how there's always a block solid antique type desk right behind those TV lawyers, all suited up with their arms folded like the big bad wolf, ready to go for the jugular and win you lots of money. That desk is their cred. You think the ad would be as effective without the desk?"

Lewis adding, "Most food products, except the start-up delivery services, have fallen off the radar, too."

"You're both correct," I told them.

Because... at this moment in time— our sole paying market is ear swabs.

Ear swabs are still hanging on. Despite the controversy. Bored people can turn a carrot into a cause célèbre.

Now the anti-swab base is gearing up claiming the swab shoves the wax further into the drum. I have yet to see any scientific evidence to support this jargon. Not even a lousy X-ray showing wax globules clinging deep inside, eventually causing hearing loss.

What I have seen— protesters carrying big signs shaped like ears. Some have the swab hanging out like the ear is smoking a cigarette. Marches down Main Street U.S.A. as well as here in the city, from north to south on the Avenues, across the Brooklyn Bridge (tying up traffic for hours) and plenty more. Plenty of anger and shouting. What if it was something serious? Who ties up the Brooklyn Bridge for cancer?

It's all gotten to Janice. Lately she's been worried about the baby's ears and how to clean them. I feel she is holding this against me personally. I want to say: *Should there be a baby.*

Of course the network mongrels lost no time jumping on the bandwagon. Then, when I thought things couldn't get worse, up pops an Indie Short from a college film studies program. You cruise the TV for something soothing and this is the shit you get. Someone actually made a black and white film about a relationship ending over whether or not to use an ear swab. The husband-actor digging out the wax with his fingernail, in a pathetic attempt to appease this (actress) woman he loves, while she, of course, is portrayed as radically anti-swab. And frankly she's not all that attractive in the black and white medium. I suppose they figured it would be too gross in color what with the wax. Or maybe they were going for the cool element. Black and white can give you a big edge in distribution. At any rate, he dug it out and stared at the wax for some time before he pulled out of that relationship, too.

⁂

Janice is falling apart. In an attempt to divert her mind off the baby stuff, I convinced her to watch a TV drama about Beethoven. She's a big classical music buff. I made microwave popcorn and we sat close on the roomy couch. It was really surprising to learn how uncouth Beethoven was, lifting his tunic to take a crap in front of his char woman. Beethoven seemed to get away with a lot of bad behavior simply on account of his genius. Naturally him being deaf was a big angle in the plot.

"It could have been simple ear wax," I said to Janice when it was over. "A mere twirl of the swab and his life might have been totally different. Imagine that!"

Constantly chilly, she was draped in a crocheted afghan granny blanket of primary colors in that squared-off pattern— the kind volunteers used to make for hospital patients— when it was safe to have anything from the outside world inside the ICU. I believe her mother crocheted it during Janice's teen years and she took it away with her to college. I reached out tugging on an end, trying to flirt a little.

"How about this?" I tugged the afghan in a second attempt. "If Beethoven was able to hear right up to the end of his life, do you think the notes of his Ninth Symphony would have still banged around inside his head? Maybe he would've gone another direction musically. Composing in an altogether different style."

"Rap."

When Janice turned bitter there was nothing to be done.

I took the empty popcorn bowl to the kitchen, rinsed it, still musing over Beethoven. How such a slob could turn out such magnificent music. I'm sure his fingernails were long and unkempt; they should have been able to dig out a sufficient amount of wax. If that is what caused his deafness. Of course he probably had syphilis, too; they all did back then. And without penicillin...

If a doctor in those times had offered Beethoven penicillin would he have taken the shot? I say unlikely. Things haven't changed all that much in 200 years.

When I went back to the living room Janice was sound asleep on the couch wrapped in her teenage afghan. I listened to her quiet breathing a moment before taking myself to bed.

Frankly, on the evolutionary scale, I don't see much forward movement in human beings. You market products for most of your adult life, you learn the absolute necessity of including the human factor. Mandatory. It uses up a lot of brain time. What will these humans like or dislike? How do they want it served up? Fish in their fudge?

CHAPTER 6

The Boss – The Icing Stick

At headquarters in Chicago they're exploring other avenues for the swab. The most recent as a cake decorating tool. That ended in a thud.

During testing, the cotton swabbing unraveled and stuck to the icing. Plus, it was impossible to fashion a decent icing flower using the swab. The pitch was aimed at the *Betty Crocker stay at home type moms (or dads)* who've been baking up a storm since their favorite bakeries shuttered. Unfortunately the icing stick was a bust. Betty Crocker and the other cake companies have been selling ready-to-go icing in convenient size cans with handy snap lids for quite some time. Our front line people did not do a good job researching. Who the hell could be bothered attempting homemade when you can just pop a lid? And, yada yada.

Then the lawyers got involved— more yada: The wooden stick could potentially splinter into miniscule slivers choking a person (even causing death). / At the very least it could cause considerable (legal) damage to the esophagus and surrounding area. / At baby's first birthday party the icing could potentially be hiding stick material and cotton swabbing which could cause a child / and, or, untold numbers of children to get sick (or even die). Why they chose to emphasize the first birthday party is anyone's guess.

And, that was the short list.

When the lawyers got finished wiping the floor with us, the horrors inflicted by the icing stick rivalled Hiroshima.

Consequently, the consultant prior to DeGrande was fired. As it was *his brilliant idea*. I don't recall his name.

❖

It's an ear swab. There's only so much we can do. Soft cotton padded tips wound on both ends of a thin stick. I suppose some people do prefer to pick their ears clean. It has worked down the centuries. Maybe we should all give up toilet paper. Leaves worked down through the centuries, too. DeGrande had better come up with a fresh take. That's why he's being paid. Not to hang around pontificating about belly buttons and lording it over the rest of these people. DeGrande had better put on his thinking cap fast.

CHAPTER 7

The Boss – Idea

Today when I walk in DeGrande charges me like a hungry fox. "Boss, I'm really stoked you're hip to my idea," he says.

"Yes, yes. But don't get too worked up, it still needs to be tested."

Quinn and Kenny jump right in wanting to know what is the new idea. What I want to know is why they're always sniffing around when they could be doing something about resuscitating the swab!

Because I have no clue what DeGrande is talking about I tell them, "DeGrande will bring you up to snuff." Then I clap him on the back.

CHAPTER 8

The Employee – Options

Sandra or Cassandra has quit for reasons unknown. Tanya says the Boss knows why. But he's not in the office. I'm thinking the false eyelashes give her look a violent edge. This morning there's been lots of chat. Tanya says the new consultant DeGrande knows. He says he doesn't know. He's probably been screwing her. That identical bright deceit flickers in both their eyes. Maybe the Cassandras got wind of something big and they quit. I've been out of the loop.

After the XMAS bash I stayed home to work. Never got to officially meet her— them— the Cassandras. I only came back because the Boss phoned and asked me to. Here I am. I don't see a red carpet welcome.

The ones still left are slumped in chairs in front of a widescreen. Everyone looking listless. "Where's Quinn?" I say.

"Called to Ireland by his tribesmen," says DeGrande.

No Quinn and no Boss.

"I find that a superior attitude," I tell DeGrande.

He smiles like a killer. Everything feels violent and unchained.

"When is Quinn coming back?" It's freaky to even think this... but I miss his burly kindness.

"Quinn? Unlikely," says DeGrande.

"How long you been working here?"

"A while. I've been put in charge." He coughs. "Temporarily. Until the Boss is back."

Hm. Very temporarily is my guess. Unless the Boss quits or his plane goes down in Havana.

"I'll have to give Quinn a call," I say. Let this DeGrande know Quinn is a Mate.

Quinn. So totally crazy with his Waterford Crystal and all that; but a Mate just the same. I can sense this DeGrande weaving his web wherever he finds a convenient joint. Like where Tanya's legs meet at the top. She always struck me as being a little on the skeevy side; like maybe she powders her pits instead of washing them.

"So where exactly is the Boss?" I say.

"Had to fly to Chicago," says DeGrande.

"I thought he'd go by wagon train."

"Clever come-back."

"Business or pleasure?" I say.

"Pleasure in Chicago in the winter?"

They all laugh. Hardy har har.

I point at the widescreen. "What's *that* about?"

The small group of them exchange glances. It's like a geometry puzzle: the short looking up at the taller, and vice versa, some looking behind their backs one way, then the other direction.

Finally Tanya speaks up. "It had a purpose at first. A purpose of enjoyment. Now it's been locked down to medical info shit only. If I had known..."

Aha! Lockdown. The Boss doesn't suffer fools lightly.

"What's in the bag?" DeGrande points at my bulging knapsack. "I see you carry The Northface."

The guy is quick. He moved the conversation away from Tanya. Confirming my suspicions. Is the brand name I lug around any of his concern? I drop it onto an empty desk. "I carry my own food and water, if that's what you mean. So there's no guesswork."

He's nodding, nodding, real serious; taking in my curt reply like a survivalist manifesto.

"And what might that guesswork be?" he says having the last word.

The guy has an odd face. Flat with a very small nose. Almost no bridge. Possibly the smallest that will still allow for air flow, allow a person to breathe on his own. A flat pancake with two holes is the best way to describe his face. My mom used to cook pancakes for breakfast when we were kids. She wouldn't flip until the raw side was totally covered in tiny air holes. Staring at DeGrande's flat mug I start to chuckle thinking *If that's plastic surgery, I hope you got your money back.*

"Something strike your funny bone?"

"Nope. Just deciding." I pat my knapsack. "Do I want P&J for lunch with the Sarah Beth Strawberry-Rhubarb spreadable fruit on fresh bakery white? Or the baked ham and imported Swiss on seeded rye with Country Dijon. I have options. My options are always open."

"We all have options," says DeGrande.

While I was working from home I got hooked on those daytime Noir films up on the high channels. That black and white hit me on a level. It hits me now that he could play any one of the murderers. That face! And how he holds himself both stiff and wiry at the same time. Like from any stationary position he could spring into action and shiv you on a dime.

"No, we don't all have options," I say.

I don't say *haven't you noticed*? Half the damn world hasn't a single decent option. I also don't say *I think your's might be running out*. I noticed a tension when he spoke of the Boss though he tried sounding flip. As a decoy I offer him a sandwich of his choice.

"Thanks, man, that's very cool of you to give up an option. But I already made lunch plans."

"Your decision," I say.

He wants to shake on it.

"Elbow bump is better," I say.

"It's a sad world."

"Tell me about it."

CHAPTER 9

The Employee – Bo-Peep

Chicago is snowed in solid for a week. The Boss still gone. De-Grande is flexing his temporary boss muscles at every opportunity.

"Gather ye 'round," he's calling out. "But remember to keep your 6 foot safety zone. Bring your chair to my office."

There's some confusion— which office? — nobody seems to know DeGrande has an office. Or where in this very long room that office might be located.

He claps to get our attention. "I'm in the Boss's office. Temporarily," he says. "For expediency. There's a working phone in there. A red landline. Cool, right! And obviously I can't keep running in and out every time there's an important call on the Boss's special red land line."

"That makes sense," says Tanya. Protecting her turf and surf? Heh heh.

In one day DeGrande has hired two women to replace the Cassandras. Both new ones are attractive. When I told him I believed it was *only one* who actually quit, he explained: *This way we'll have a replacement if the other new one leaves.*

"It's a topsy turvy work environment," he told me. "We need to improvise wherever possible."

⁂

Doing plenty of bitching and moaning, people are dragging their chairs all the way back there, someone running a chair leg over someone's ankle, a little blood is shed. It turns out we all can't fit in the Boss's office and still maintain the 6 foot buffer zone.

"We'll have to improvise," says DeGrande.

Again with the improvising. Is that all he's got in his bag of tricks?

"Life is about improvising," he goes on.

Again!!!

"You try something it doesn't work you go on to the next best. If you sit around crying and complaining your life will end with a splat rather than a wild explosion of fireworks." He's beaming like what he said is worthy of Shakespeare.

All in all, not a good speech. One of the new-hire Cassandra replacements, a short perky blonde with a Dutch girl haircut, bursts out crying. Her mother, it seems, passed from the virus a few months earlier. She calls her *Mama* with a French accent as she cries her heart out. The girls gather around, giving her distanced air hugs, with their arms extended flapping like wings.

After a few minutes of this DeGrande sort of flips out. "People, people, distance please! Distance!" Of course it has no effect on the girls who are now patting her head. I assume they assume the virus has no interest in hair.

DeGrande finally goes into the Boss's office, sits in the Boss's chair and throws up his hands.

When the girl stops crying she marches into the Boss's office calling DeGrande an insensitive asshole then she storms out. "What did I tell you?" he says to me. "Improvise! It was the right decision hiring two of them."

I kind of liked that girl. Her corn color hair cut short and swingy really lifted my mood. Other things lately are having a similar affect. I saw a coffee mug advertised in a magazine that had a cartoon of an old skinny guy doing some kind of calisthenics. The coffee mug lingo read: *Lean Mean Aging Machine.* I don't have a clue why that would uplift me. In any case, there goes my little Bo-Peep (I decide she's a definite Bo-Peep type minus the curls and staff). Gone before I ever found out her real name.

"What was her name?" I say to Lewis who's putting his chair next to mine.

"This freakin' guy is going to wreck the whole office," Lewis says. "The Boss better get back here."

"I have nothing to do with it."

"Did I say you did?"

Quinn and only Quinn would know how to handle this DeGrande jerk-off. Whenever things got hot and hairy, he always threatened to round up his old IRA pals. So old, probably most of them already kicked the bucket. Still— it's good to work with a guy who has a temper well hidden under his skin— to be taken out only when a temper is required. Lewis, on the other hand, is a light-weight. He doesn't fool me for a second. He's trying to stir me into becoming like Quinn; a substitute Quinn. Deep down Lewis is a coward.

I poke my head in the Boss's office. "Is the meeting still on?" I ask DeGrande.

"Of course it's on! This is a place of business and will continue to be under my watch." Then he comes out into the main space.

I can hear Stella and Allie making snarky noises behind cupped hands.

"Everyone sit down out here," DeGrande is saying, spreading his arms wide. "Lots of room out here. Plenty of room for everyone." Smiling like it's a barbecue and the grill is fired up.

Sluggishly, people move their chairs again. They liked Bo-Peep. She had an innocence. Now the day is marked by another cloud burst.

"Make a wide semi-circle," he's saying, "and we'll pick up where we left off. Chop Chop!" All smiles and good will; like any moment champagne corks are gonna pop.

CHAPTER 10

The Employee – Beautification

The Boss has come back from Headquarters in a bad mood. He sits in his office all day, hardly speaks to any of us unless we come knocking. He does manage to fire DeGrande later in the week by calling it a lay-off. Blaming it on the slowness of things. Then the Boss stays home a few days.

Everyone has an opinion. Maybe it's the thing to do. Act like a miserable asshole, get ratted out to the Boss, get yourself canned. Collect unemployment. Then every imaginable obstacle re unemployment is raised: It won't pay the rent where I live / I won't be able to afford my dog walker / I'll have to give up Whole Foods / I like my sheets ironed by hand from the Chinese laundry. And on and on and on.

Compared with this bunch, I live frugally. On restaurant dates (pre-pandemic) I made it clear we each pay our own food and drinks. Women want equal rights but that doesn't seem to include the restaurant bill. Some have argued hard over paying their share. One ran out sticking me with the bill. Also, I do not have my sheets ironed, and the cheaper supermarkets and bodegas work fine for me. I use any discount coupons, and save a few bucks a week by bringing my lunch to work.

In the middle of this controversy over whether to get canned, something occurs to me. "Hey!" I have to yell to be heard over the racket. "What about the last person left? The one who hasn't been fired or quit? And has no way out?"

The room grows quiet. Then all eyes turn on Tanya as she starts to speak. "I'll take the risk and be the odd woe-man out."

"You're joking, right?" I say. She's willing to be the last resistance fighter left in the building?

"It's not a joke. I don't care. The last person here will become the new Boss. Don't you see? You think our Boss is going to hang in as his people leave one at a time? He's got his own problems at home." Adding in a dreamy voice, "I've always wanted to be Boss."

The widescreen has been airing a medi-fomercial on liver disease. I noticed, then got sidetracked by this discussion. A dark line on the screen is indicating how many drinks per day = liver wreckage. In my opinion, they should have made the drinks look dark and dreary. The drinks sparkle with colorful effervescence. Who could resist?

"Tanya, I think you have a client back there waiting to get in your beauty parlor," says Lewis. "Aren't you boss of that?"

"Fuck you," she says, strutting off in her stilettos.

Why does it always have to end in a fuck you?

‡

I may go home. My neck is so damn itchy. I noticed in the Mens Room mirror a few red bumps this morning. From the so-called cashmere scarf I bought for twenty bucks at the XMAS Fair on West Broadway? I questioned the woman selling the scarves but in a nice way: *You can sell cashmere scarves for twenty dollars and still make a profit?* I tossed it off lightly. She didn't take it lightly. I should've been forewarned. I scratch again.

"You're gouging your skin," says Stella. "Want some of my Aloe cream?"

"Is it soothing?"

"Yes. It also has hemp."

Lewis says, "Can we smoke it?"

Then what walks in but a Golden Retriever followed by no other than Quinn. The old timers make a huge fuss while the few new hires watch in boredom keeping their distance. Quinn grabs me by the neck shaking me. "Good to see you, Mate!"

Aaaahhh... not the neck...

"You as well, Mate," I manage to croak out before he lets go. "We were just the other day talking about you. Thought you'd never come back."

"Bollocks! You shoulda placed a few bets." Quinn all jolly in voice and demeanor.

Despite the neck which feels much worse now I'm really happy to see him. So much so I start to quiver. I'm having this weird visceral response to him. Nothing sexual. Returned to the fold at last, Quinn is one of the few people I can count on. Realizing it is sobering. "Big turnover lately," I tell him keeping it low key.

He scans the small group. "Tanya gone?" He's sporting a mid-length scruffy white beard. Swiping a hand under his nose and looking around like Tanya is about to jump out saying *boo!*

"She's still here." I crank my thumb. "Back there— at her beautification station."

He repeats *beautification station* and lets out a big belly laugh. Hearing the laughter fires up the dog who barks happily sort of chasing its tail. One of those perpetually cheerful dogs. Quinn has it all spiffed up in a plaid dog jacket and matching collar with tags and such.

"Tanya's making the world a more beautiful place," I say. "Well some of the world." Why am I going on about her?

I don't go on to tell him what I really feel— this tug in my chest all the time; how deep down I'm constantly lonely. And that I believe I could've made a go of things with Bo-Peep. I just say, "Mate, it's damned good to see you."

Eye to eye we knuckle bump.

"Hey! We should do another bash, what with Valentine's Day right around the bend. I got my Waterford punchbowl in the car. Should I bring it in for storage?"

"You think it will be safe here when everyone leaves for the night and on the weekends?"

"Safer than the car," Quinn says. "I had a time of it back home. Thieves broke into my ancient Renault and stole my clothes." He rubs his beard, seems to be pondering the incident. "Broad daylight. I only stopped for a quick pint."

Everyone has gathered to hear his story of Ireland. Stella, on her knees, is rubbing the dog's ears, the dog making sweet sounds at her.

"I almost didn't come back," he says into my ear. "I fell in love in that pub. Mad love. Sheilah. Black hair, black eyes, that silken olive skin. To die for. Whenever I call her *Black Irish* she wants to throttle me."

"What is black Irish?"

"A legend that the Spaniards came over in big ships to plunder Ireland, leaving their dark beauty mark." He shrugs. "Who knows and who's complaining? We met that very day those thieves stole my duds from the car."

CHAPTER 11

The Employee – Quinn In Love

"Love can drive you straight to heaven or hell. There is no in between with love. The kind that eats your skin to the bone and makes you shine like the death apple." Quinn orates as he putters around with his desk.

"Did you just make that up?" I say.

"Nah. Got it off those inspirational internet cards. I send Sheilah one every day. She loves them. They cement us while I'm gone."

"I never heard of the death apple."

"One of those Adam and Eve things," he says. "Catholic, all that."

Again, the Boss hasn't come in. The girls are mostly at the widescreen drinking various juices concocted from a deluxe juicer Tanya ordered off HSN. I have no idea where Lewis has gotten off to. Half the time I can't remember who works here. The girl who was hired along with Bo-Peep, some Emma, has been home with a head cold. Let's hope that's all she's got going.

"Will you be bringing Sheilah to The States?" I ask Quinn.

"She hates Americans. Says they're cheap tippers and cause big problems in the pub when they come through Ireland in the tour groups."

He's in love with a woman who hates Americans. How will that work out? "Will you be living with her in Ireland, then?"

"I'll never go back to stay."

"Well, how will this be arranged?"

"Same as any other love affair. You see her when you get the time to steal away. Usually from your wife." He laughs heartily and takes two cigars from his top pocket shaking them at me. "From a big do for my sister's new bub— drinks, eats, cigars, the works. I saved one each for us, to smoke together when I got back."

It feels good knowing he thought enough of me as a Mate to save me a cigar from his family gathering. I no longer feel connected to this city. The people I knew from the outside have split for the country or moved to another state. One guy, Paulo, to New Zealand. It's a lonely city when you don't have people here and there for a drink, a movie, a Saturday bagel.

"Let's take this in the Boss's office," Quinn says. To the dog he says, "Come along, Pretzel."

‡

In the two client chairs facing the Boss's desk we cut the ends with Quinn's special cigar knife and light up.

"Remember when the Boss always had clients in these chairs," says Quinn blowing smoke rings. "Those were good days." After a little while he stands up. "Think I'll borrow the Boss's chair. See how it feels smoking a cigar like it feels to the Boss."

Sooner or later everyone borrows the Boss's chair. Not me; not yet.

"I like the swivel action," he says twirling in the chair.

"Enjoy yourself."

We puff in silence. Restful. In a corner Pretzel seems to be snoozing. No one is shouting, complaining, putting someone down; and the widescreen is too far away to even know it exists.

"You have a picture of Sheilah?"

"On my mobile." He grins handing it over, and I'm staring at this beautiful woman with her head thrown back, her long olive-skinned neck looking graceful as a portrait painting. Hair that's true black. Not like that dyed black mop of Tanya's. I'm relieved to be able to tell Quinn the honest truth; that Sheilah is very beautiful.

"One of you has to give in on which country," I say. "You don't want to lose this woman."

He laughs in sputters. "It's all been arranged. My brothers and I bought the pub and the land. Now I own her. It's better than a marriage."

"I don't get it. She can just leave and go to any other pub."

"That's right. Technically. But she won't. It's Ireland. Her people have been going to that pub a hundred or more years. My pub, now. She'll stay put. When I want to see her I get on a plane and suffer the mask. Trust me, Mate."

It all sounds odd but what do I know? "I hope you know what you're doing."

His smoke rings come out pretty expertly. "Soon we'll bring the feckin' punch bowl in." He grins like a Cheshire Cat. "And the little cups to match."

CHAPTER 12

The Boss – Flowers

I pause at the flower stand on Second Avenue, the one I pass every night walking home. A bright spot in this sea of darkness. Janice loves flowers. A fresh bunch might crack that sheet of ice, growing thicker, between us. Should I or shouldn't I? It's freezing temps but they look OK. Must be the heat lamps hanging over the bleacher style racks. Flower bleachers. College football games spring to mind. The good old days. Cheer Leaders in short pleated skirts and Pom-Pom girls. Me in my white # 21 jersey. Ancient history.

So, flowers. If Janice were picking out a bunch she'd be bending and sniffing, checking to see the little green stem cups (she has a botanical name for them) are squeezed tight cupping the flower base. If they lay back like they're lounging they've given up the ghost— you can betcha it's an old flower near its expiration date. Tonight I'm feeling pretty old myself.

The wind off the avenue comes whipping around the corner. It's too cold to stand here inspecting. I grab a bunch of deep-pink roses dripping water from the rubber container.

"Hey!" I say to the guy sitting on a turned-over bucket. Every night he's out here freezing his ass off and still manages a friendly smile. He stops cutting thorns off rose stems to make change. "Keep it," I say.

He salutes me. A warm feeling spreads through my chest. What the hell? It's only a five dollar tip. No one has saluted me since the war. The war—quick as the warmth came over it dissolves. And that's with two + beers in my belly. Who's counting? Anyway it's too cold to linger and chat. I'm doubtful the guy speaks enough English to be conversational. Clutching the dripping bouquet, I salute him back with my other hand; then turning the corner move toward home. *Home is where the heart is.*

When we first got married, Janice stitched in needlepoint a thing-a-ma-jig with those words wrapped around a cornucopia basket she also stitched. Overflowing with needlepoint fruit. Framed, it hangs in our galley kitchen. I haven't noticed it lately. Then, again, haven't looked.

CHAPTER 13

The Employee – Red Spread

Around five-ish, huffing from the weight of the punchbowl Quinn shoves it under a desk. "It's feckin' freezing out there. Any newspapers lying about?"

"What for?"

"Just bring all you can find."

I return with a stack that's been moldering in the supply closet.

"This must be five years' worth," he says chucking them on top of the punchbowl. "Best to hide it. It is Waterford, after all. Pawn shop would sell it for a pretty penny."

Mario, the head doorman, appears holding a cardboard box.

"I saw the Boss last night," says Quinn, still out of breath. "Set it down here, Mario. Thanks a lot Mate."

"Anytime, Mr. Quinn."

"Oh, yeah? You saw the Boss? You two go to a bar?" I'm feeling a ping of jealous.

"You silly feck! I saw him buying blooms on the street for the Missus."

He tips Mario who fake protests. Quinn saying softly, "It's only ten quid, have one on me that goes down like silk."

Mario pockets the cash strolling away whistling.

Since his return from Ireland Quinn's lingo has modified somewhat. Quid. Mate. Feck.

"Did the Boss say he'd be coming in tomorrow?" I ask him.

"We didn't speak. I was across the street then he took off."

"If he was out buying flowers, well, it's a sure bet he'll be back here soon." Why? Why is it a sure bet? Am I losing control of reality?

With his own air of certainty Quinn says, "The Boss will come in whenever he feels up to it. That's why he's the Boss."

"Right."

I never feel up to it. Coming in. I feel beat. The widescreen is blaring another medi-fomercial. That thing has become tiresome. There's only so many jokes you can make— today psoriasis is spread across the screen.

"That's one condition you do not want to catch," Kenny says.

"Where have *you* been?" I say. "A space mission?"

"I don't think you can catch psoriasis," Stella says from behind her mask.

She's been more vocal lately. I think she's feeling her oats what with a few more recent new hires for her to lord over.

"You can get psoriasis from too much stress," she says. "I already watched this one last week."

"You mean they have repeats?"

She looks me up and down as if to say *How dumb is that*. "Not repeats, it's on a reel."

"Stress? If that's the case we should all be up to our arses in psoriasis," Quinn says looking around the room. "Where should we set up for the Valentine bash?"

Arses in psoriasis. That's a new one.

Quinn's prodding me. "Where should we set up?"

And it's like a bad dream all over again— the XMAS bash. My feelings of isolation, how the girls fawned over Quinn. But now we're Mates. That could possibly change the whole scenario.

"How did we set up last time?" He's scrabbling through his beard with his hand.

I've noticed people with new beards tend to spend time digging around in them. He seems to have forgotten we used the card table. Probably now that he's a big land owner with a pub in Ireland there's a bash every night and to him it's all one alcohol blur.

"Mate." He pokes my chest bone lightly. "Where should we set up? You losing weight?"

"I'll be right back," I say.

"How 'bout we set her up near the widescreen?"

Her? "OK."

I really don't care where he sets *her* up. I'm thinking if Bo-Peep had hung around, by now we'd have something going between us and I wouldn't have to worry about being ignored.

"Let's move it and get it over with," I say. My need to splash water on my itchy neck is fierce.

Seems Mario the doorman never actually left. He's malingering, wanders toward us, pushing up one jacket sleeve then the other. Checking.

"You should have someone check inside your arse," Quinn tells him with a straight face.

"You can get it in there?"

"Hurts like the blinkin' devil when they sprout in the dark environs."

"Don't listen to Quinn," I say laughing in spite of my agony. "He's just yankin' your chain."

Mario looks from me to Quinn, then pulls down the sleeves of his uniform. He stands straighter. "I don't think it's very funny under the circumstances. I left my door in order to help you. I could lose my job. Next time you need someone to lug your shit, hire a donkey," he says making tracks.

"Strange fellow." But Quinn's already past it; his eyes are scanning the room like twin lasers. "So my good man what shall we name this bash?"

Stella walking by pipes up. "Since it's Valentine's week we could call it The Red Spread."

"Clever, m'dear!" Quinn throws an air kiss. The girl blushes above her blue mask.

Lately she's been looking better. The fading black dye job, usually stringy, is pulled back neatly by a sparkly blue band. I notice she has on cowboy boots in varying shades of blue and brown. Kinda cool, I'm thinking; then wondering if they pinch at the toes.

"Are you from the west?" I say.

"The west side?"

"No, the wild west."

"You mean on account of my boots?"

"Well, yes."

"I'm from Sheepshead Bay. I bought these in that cowboy store on Madison, the one with all the cowboy hats and other cowboy stuff in the window. They even sell spurs. It's all legit cowboy stuff."

Spurs! Who the hell in this city needs spurs?

"I would say that qualifies you to be an official cowgirl," I tell her. What the heck! Bo-Peep is history, and Stella's looking kinda cute.

"You should see my hat." She's all steamed up over this cowgirl stuff.

"I'd like to," I tell her. "Do you have a Vaccine Pass for indoor dining?"

"Why?"

"Well... I was thinking maybe we could go to one of the quieter places, off the beaten track. Get a little early supper. Before they start to fill up. Get to know each other better."

"I'll let you know," she says.

PART TWO

CHAPTER 14

The Employee – Camouflage

Quinn's Valentine bash gets a lukewarm response. Same card table and green felt cloth, same punch bowl and little cups, same punch. The ladle has gone missing. I find that a tad odd. Personally, I think red felt would have made a better visual for enhancing the mood.

People take a cup, dip into the punch, push up their mask to sip, then wander away. There's no energy. Nobody even mentions the missing ladle; as if it's no big deal how they fill their cup.

"Was the ladle expensive?" I ask Quinn.

"You better believe it, solid crystal."

Someone has pitched an army tent half way to the rear, off to the side by the supply closet. Do we have a squatter? And next to the supply closet, of all places. Maybe stealing what they need from our supplies. Even the crystal ladle? It's suspect.

I never see anyone go near the tent, enter or leave, and no one here is talking about it. By now they've all seen its camouflage printed tarp. It's not like an empty bird cage you pass by.

"What's with the tent?"

Quinn lets out with the story. The Boss has left his wife. He's sleeping in the tent.

"The Boss!"

Quinn nods solemnly.

"Does anyone else know?"

"Of course. Who could miss a tent."

"I know that! Does anyone else know it's the Boss's tent?"

"Yeah. Pretty much all of 'em."

Why am I the last to know? And Stella hasn't responded to my early evening supper invite.

"I just assumed he was staying home," I say, " it is the normal assumption." But I feel like a jerk all the same. Last to know. The Boss in the tent is something pretty significant.

"Didn't the tent tip you off?" Quinn says.

"Not to the fact that the Boss is living there! I thought maybe another project by the girls, like they're selling safari clothes out of there. Or, even a squatter may have crossed my mind."

"A squatter? And you don't investigate?"

"It's not my place."

A long silence trails between us.

"Does his wife know?" I say finally.

"Oh, yeah. Janice encouraged it. She wanted him out of the apartment. As to where she thinks he's parked his bum, well, that I couldn't answer."

I feel in shock. Like by mistake I stuck my knife in the toaster. Quinn seems... what? Invigorated? Maybe he figures the Boss will totally flip and he'll become the new Boss. Just like that— flip of a switch or a toaster.

He did enjoy sitting in the Boss's leather chair when we had the cigars. He liked how the chair swiveled and I believe he commented on it. Now I suspect it went much further. He likes the whole Boss concept bigly.

"Her name is Janice?"

Quinn's head jerks. "Sure! Everyone knows Janice."

"I don't."

He laughs then and fake-punches me a few times on the arm. "You're a quiet bugger. You listen all the time, I can hear you listening. But you have to look, too." He scoops punch into a clean crystal cup, shoving it at me. "Here, have another."

"I already have a cup." Now who isn't looking?

I'm sorta pissed. A lot. If we're Mates, why wasn't I the first to know details about Janice and the tent? And more specifically *the Boss inside the tent*!!! I'm feeling jittery. This bash turned out to be a bomb. All those clean sparkling cups unused. Nobody took pictures. "It's a quieter bash than the XMAS one." It's all I can think to say.

Quinn's acting casual. "Nothing beats XMAS."

CHAPTER 15

The Employee – Cowgirl

Suddenly the tent has become a source of interest. Or maybe it was all along and I had tapped out. You pass by this person or that, you hear snippets: Has anyone seen the Boss enter or leave? How does he get his food? And the big one: his bathroom issues. If Quinn knows, he's not telling.

Now with the Boss living nearby in the tent, Quinn stays clear of the Boss's office. Being the first to leave at night. More than a few times he's mentioned the latest reopening of The Oyster Bar, adding, "The Boss loves The Oyster Bar."

How would you know that?

"It's full of tourists right now," he's saying, "but the tables are well-spaced apart. You should take your cowgirl there some weekend."

My cowgirl? Is he fucking with me?

I just say, "Is it better there on the weekend?"

"Hm?"

"You just mentioned me taking Stella there on a weekend."

I can see his gears grinding. He says, "It's special to take a woman out on the weekend." He scrunches through his beard with his hand. "You know. Like she's your special gal, not some bird you take out for a lark after work. If you get my drift. Stella's looking very fine these days, very fine indeed."

My eyes narrow. This is all total bullshit but I don't know why.

Changing the subject I say, "Today might be the day. The day the Boss steps out from the tent."

"I wouldn't bet on it."

Shrill sounds from the beauty parlor area interrupt our conversation. You get a few women together things can turn pretty noisy. As more offices are starting to re-open in the building, Tanya is getting an increase in customers. Someone ripped down her lobby sign but word of mouth spreads fast in these high-rise work environments. Plus Tanya is strict about handwashing and her KN95 mask rule. Extra masks on a hook for any customer who may have forgotten to bring one.

‡

Later in the afternoon, feeling sort of light-headed, I mention The Oyster Bar to Stella. What the heck! She informs me she's vegan. This from a girl who wears leather cowboy boots? Maybe she's one of those *exception people*; they have their strong beliefs but make exceptions for certain items or circumstances.

"I guess the cowboy boots are an exception?"

She places her hand on the card table, leaning, staring at me. So far nobody has taken the table down or even talked about removing it. Things keep getting chucked there. Like we're filling up for the losses. In this office we now have the additions of the beauty station, the widescreen, the clothing boutique, the tent, and this card table. With the green felt cloth. The heavy crystal punch bowl left a deep circular impression. A sink hole crosses my mind. A place to fall into and hang out until things somehow change. Maybe that's what the Boss is up to in the tent.

I say to Stella, "I'm sure The Oyster Bar has salad. Or whatever else you consider to be vegan food."

"Consider? I know what is vegan and what isn't." Her voice has risen significantly. I picture her kicking some cowboy in the nuts. A week or so ago she did mention spurs with a sort of affection. She starts toward the back of the room and I follow anyway.

Because there's nothing to lose, now, I shout, "Take your cowboy boots, for instance. Leather. That's from cows. Are you aware?"

She stops in the vicinity of the tent. When I catch up, she says, "You're *assuming* they're leather. Men and their dangerous assumptions. That's why we're all living in hell. Men!"

Who would've guessed she had these thoughts simmering?

"I'm sorry if I upset you." I start to back away.

"If?" she screams.

"Jesus!"

"My boots happen to be made out of vegan leather!"

Vegan leather? Half veggies half cow? "I never heard of that."

"Now you have!" she screams again. Taking a few ominous steps in my direction. Is she going to hit me?

"What's all the commotion?" The Boss. He's finally out.

CHAPTER 16

The Employee – Hiya

The Boss is back. Sort of. Outside the tent he stumbles getting his bearings. It's like watching a toddler take the first steps. If the Boss falls in the middle of the afternoon— which in this city already looks like dusk what with skyscrapers everywhere blocking the low winter sun— that will be a degrading moment for the Boss. I don't know if I should rush to his aid.

"Hiya," says the Boss but more of a croak. The few people nearby look stunned and sort of mutter back their shocked hellos.

The Boss has never said *hiya* to anyone in all the time I've worked here. *Hiya* isn't his style. That they look shocked strikes me funny. Did they expect after weeks in a tent he'd come out wearing his cool black leather bomber jacket and fake-worn jeans? Less reality than ever here pumping through people.

Then the Boss says, "How're you all doing?" Just like before. I take this as a good sign.

When no one answers he looks from person to person. "Doing pretty good, Boss," I say breaking the ice. "Under the circumstances."

He nods. As if he comprehends his predicament. A moment later he's focused on his arm which he picks at. I wonder if he's ever cleaned up in the Mens Room once the office emptied out for the night? Does he have a cot in the tent? A sleeping bag? How did he take a poop during the day? – when the office had employees and the girls had customers. So many questions. In his rumpled smelly condition I think of an anthropologist who spent a long time living with baboons.

There seems to be nothing else to say. He looks up a few times; appears unfocused; except when it comes to his arm which he picks till it bleeds. I ask, "Can I get you a band-aid, Boss?"

He's wiping the blood on his sweat pants. I decide it's best to leave him be. Let him get a feel for the office without everyone scrutinizing him. When I start to move away, the rest of them follow. Not because I'm a person of power and influence here. Because they don't want to get involved. Too messy.

I head out and down to the lobby for The Post, running into Quinn by the elevators. "The Boss has come out," I say.

Quinn looks red and puffy, like after a hard night of drinking.
"So he's back. In all his glory?"
"If you could call it that."
Quinn barely acknowledges.
"Don't be shocked," I say.
"Nothing shocks me, Mate."

‡

In the roughly ten minutes it took me to ride the elevator down,
go to the newsstand, buy a paper, then ride back up, the office is
complete turmoil.

The Boss is sobbing. Tanya put a call through to the wife and
she didn't pick up. Everyone is trying to calm him which isn't
working. I'm embarrassed for the Boss. Such a steep fall from
grace for a man who appeared to have everything. I guess under
certain conditions anyone can crack. At times I've felt at odds,
myself. Quinn, seeing the Boss in this state, tries giving him a
shoulder rub which the Boss shakes off violently. "Only Justine
lays a hand on me!" the Boss screams.

There are whispers: *Should we call 911?*

What the hell went on in that tent, day after day, night after
night?

"No 911." I say this firmly. I have their full attention. "You
want the Boss put in the psych ward at Bellevue?" Heads are
shaking, nobody wants to see that happen. "We have to get hold
of Janice, somehow," I say. "Does anyone have a landline number
to their apartment?"

Negative.

I can understand the filth of him, and his confusion. But it's
like the Boss has morphed into another entity. Another being.
A half-man. The baboon image crosses my mind again. Is the
Boss caught up in some evolutionary mis-step? A moment later
I'm thinking *Who will become the new boss?* And another strange
thing— the Boss hasn't lost any weight that I can see. His dirty
sweats cling to a belly bulge. What has he been eating? From
where? Before the tent, the Boss had a washboard belly.

Deep guttural sounds come out as he sobs for Janice. I can't
stand seeing the Boss this way.

"Someone try her number again!" Quinn screams. "Or go
stake out the apartment until she returns."

Quinn offers to go get the Boss food. It doesn't seem to register with the Boss. Someone suggests we take a peek in the tent. No one dares step forward; I'm certainly not about to. The tent is the Boss's private domain. No matter what. This is a Boss I do not know. This is a creature. I feel terrible thinking such a thing about the Boss. He was always, as my mom used to say, *a real decent kind of man.*

Then one of the girls says, *Why are his hands orange?* Opinions and suggestions fly fast and furious.

A panic goes up when Lewis suggests it could be a new variant.

"We already have an O," Quinn says. "Orange hands do not equal a new variant."

Nevertheless, people begin to space apart and double down on their masking. The Boss isn't wearing one and refuses the pristine white K95 Stella offers, bashing it away with his orange hand. She looks horrified.

"I wonder if other parts of his body have gone orange?" I mutter to Quinn.

"It's feckin' unsettling," Quinn says. "I'm not about to check his body."

"I heard that," says Lewis creeping up behind us. What is it about this place that makes people turn so paranoid? Lewis's eyes are bugging. "Maybe we *should* phone for an ambulance. Now that he's out of the tent he could spread this orange variant to any one of us. Or all of us," Lewis says.

"We've been through that!" I say.

A beauty customer who wandered over has picked up on talk of this latest possible health crisis. "What if this new orange one turns out to make long term covid?" the woman says.

"Look at it this way, dearie," says Quinn. "You won't have to fly to the Caribbean to get a nice orange glow."

Some hesitant laughter, then the customer calls Quinn a jackass. But his joke kind of lowers the temperature. People are looking slightly less freaked. Are they actually considering this new orange as a possible *good* side effect?

As if reading my thoughts, Stella says, "They keep telling us to embrace the positive in all this misery. I've looked high and low. An orange glow would work for me." She studies her hand as if picturing a glowing tan.

All this talk going on as if the Boss disappeared again; which he hasn't; standing here steadily picking his arm. It's terrible. Like the Boss is just some object in their retail palace. Another tall vase to fill with flowers. I want to approach the Boss and talk to him quietly. But I know it will be useless because the Boss is travelling in another zone.

Tanya groans. "No one is turning orange." One eye on her phone, she's watching the time. "I have a customer getting highlights," she says to no one in particular.

Another beauty customer comes over. "I'm Tanka and I'm here for color, too. If anyone is an expert on color it's Tanya."

Tanya and Tanka. Fuck! It's like the Cassandras come back to life. Just another day. To them the Boss isn't even here. Bleeding.

CHAPTER 17

The Employee – Survive

The day drags on. The Boss is still out and picking. Tanya's high heels click-click-clicking toward the reception area where she bends under the counter. Comes up with a bag of Cheetos. "Only one bag under here," she says. "I keep stocking them yet it goes down so fast. I was wondering who could be devouring so many bags? My Cheetos orders have tripled since the Boss took up tent life."

Quinn says, "A person can't survive on Cheetos."

"Well?" says Tanya raising an eyebrow.

Meanwhile Lewis is down on his back across one of the empty desks, legs dangling over the plexiglass divider. "I don't know how much more I can take."

Quinn says, "If you think you'd be happier working elsewhere…"

Like a ventriloquist dummy whose strings got pulled Lewis sits up in one quick motion. "Who died and made *you* Boss?"

"I'm the Boss!" roars the Boss. "I'm calling a meeting. Everyone in my office in five minutes."

CHAPTER 18

The Employee – Meeting

Back there we can't all fit in his office. We realized that when DeGrande called a meeting in the Boss's office when the Boss was away. But no one dares tell the Boss for fear it might set him off again. People are muttering *useless useless*— dragging chairs down the whole length of the room and for what?

"I wonder why he didn't set up his home away from home back here near his office," Lewis says.

I find that pretty damned insensitive. Obviously the Boss is having a breakdown of sorts. I almost want to cry for what has become of the Boss.

Tanya has to go wash out her dye job customer. She says, "Tell the Boss I'm in the bathroom and I'll be back as soon as I can."

I give her the thumbs up. She's been nicer to me lately.

Everyone is standing around with their chair. As if they picked up a twin along the route. Nobody wants to go inside the office. Finally Quinn taps then opens the door sticking his head in, pulling it out. "No Boss here."

It creates a huge stir. Where could he have gone? Is this his idea of a joke? Maybe he's still confused and thinks he belongs in the other small office? Then Quinn says, "Do you think he meant a meeting in another building?"

People shout down that last suggestion. Quinn holds his ground. "He used to leave here for long stretches of time. Maybe he's been sneaking around playing at more than one job. And that's why he slept *here*. To be close by to both. He may have gotten confused about which place he'd be having the meeting."

This mounts another uproar.

You, of all people, I'm thinking glaring at Quinn. *You* with business on both sides of the pond.

Allie starts to cry, then bolts toward the front without her chair. "I guess she's going home," says Stella.

"Look," I say. "The Boss works here and only here. I think we should give him benefit of the doubt. He's always been fair to us. Maybe he wants to clean himself up before the meeting."

A few people nod saying things like: *Yes, of course, of course he'd want to wash up.*

"All right," Quinn says. "Fifteen minutes."

"Fifteen minutes!" Kenny holds his nose. "He needs a total fumigation. That's gonna take more than a lousy fifteen minutes."

Quinn tells everyone to chill. "Give him half an hour. If he's not here by then I'm breaking out the punch bowl."

There's more shouting. "*No! No more punch! No punch!*" Lewis mentions the last punch bash giving him bowel problems.

Quinn raises both hands high. "From my punch? I think not." It's the closest to rage I've ever seen in him. It does quiet people. "You ever hear about making lemonade when life hands you lemons?" he says.

Oh, no. Does he actually think collectively we're this stupid? He's waiting for a response. Maybe we are stupid. When no one says a word, Quinn mutters, "Ya feckin' bunch of quitters."

"You know something," Lewis says to Quinn.

"What's that?"

"I don't even know your first name."

"It's Quinn."

"That's your last name."

"Your surname," says Stella.

"Right."

"Are you saying your entire name is Quinn Quinn?" from Stella again.

"No, my sweets. I am not saying that. My entire name is Quinn A period Quinn."

"A for arsehole?" says Lewis sticking it to him.

"Clever." Quinn removes a flask from his pocket. "I'd love to share with you, Mate," he says swinging the flask as if to hit Lewis. Lewis ducks. Quinn takes a long swig. "Being we got covid hovering I wouldn't want to risk infecting you. I could be an asymptomatic carrier." He drinks again, swallows, goes *ahhhh...*

Allie comes running back gasping behind the mask. "I saw the Boss go in the tent!"

Everyone getting crazy stirred up again.

"*Did he seem different?*"

"*Was he cleaned up?*"

"*Did he say anything?*"

That kind of stuff.

"Well, I did notice the orange was off his hands," says Allie.

"You saying he washed them?" says Lewis.

"Maybe he licked them clean," says Quinn. An evil cast moving into his light-blue eyes; lately always red-rimmed.

CHAPTER 19

The Employee – Cheetos

No further sightings of the Boss. After a few days everyone reconciled to the fact he reclaimed his tent home. Tanya beefs up the Cheetos orders to triple, and includes packaged meats and cheese, dried fruit, bananas, brioche rolls and orange juice. She reads the list out loud asking if anyone can think of anything else for the Boss.

Stella says, "Mayonnaise. And cookies."

"Mayo needs refrigeration once it's opened," Lewis says. "He won't remember then he'll come down with mayonnaise poisoning. It's very painful. Believe me, I know firsthand."

His bowel problems again?

"You can get mayo in those little packets," Stella says.

Lewis holds his position on mayo. "He could use half then store the other half for god knows how long."

"OK, cookies." Tanya adds them to the list. "We can't let the Boss starve or go malnourished," she says. "The Cheetos and only the Cheetos are for everyone. Get it? The rest of the stuff is for the Boss and only the Boss. Any person caught pilfering the Boss's food will be subject to extreme disciplinary action. I will personally be keeping a tight watch on the fridge and all withdrawals will be noted on my Excel spreadsheet."

Disciplinary action? How will Tanya know, for instance, exactly who ate the ham or the cheese? Or the cookies?

"Mario and his team will be installing security cameras beamed at the fridge area."

It's like she's reading my mind. I've read this can happen when people spend a great deal of time together for no particular purpose. Like being stuck in a cave, for instance, during a war. Well, good on Tanya. Because there is only so much I can do for the Boss. And I don't even know at this point what that might be.

‡

For the first time I seriously consider quitting for good. Quinn says *What's your hurry*? He says the place is a permanent vacation with an automatic paycheck each week. He has a point. He tells me to go skiing. "Not my thing," I say.

But I feel at odds with this set up. Even though it's mostly quiet except when the girls get a customer, and around the wide-screen. That tent sitting there every day — is really getting to me.

The girls have taken this as a golden opportunity. *TANYA'S BEAUTY SPOT* (the official name) has taken off. She's hired that obnoxious customer Tanka to answer the phone. Apparently it's ringing off the hook— they're busy, busy, busy.

Quinn says, "It's nice to see the girls doing so well."

"Tanya and Tanka. Sounds like a weird cult."

"I dig Tanka as a name," Quinn says. "Primitive appeal." He winks. "I'll betcha she's got a few good moves in the sack."

What about his great love, Sheilah, back in Ireland? What about her moves in the sack? He doesn't talk much about her lately. I want to inquire but decide not to.

Meanwhile, Stella and Allie are busy setting up a clothing boutique with racks along the wall opposite and north of the tent; leaving plenty of distance. Good idea! Suppose some customer assumes that the tent, with its camouflage pattern, is an off-shoot of the boutique featuring safari-style clothes. Banana Republic did that in the very beginning, with all the camo clothes, jammed with tropical plants, drums and wild animal sounds coming from hidden speakers. It was excellent promo. The customer may remember it, wandering into the tent to have a look-see. The Boss face to face with a customer— too hideous to contemplate.

The girls are cheery hanging up the used designer stuff they buy from some outlet then plan on selling as brand new. To freshen the clothes they bought a professional standing steamer from a dry cleaner going out of business. Lately they've been strutting around like twin peacocks. You'd think they were setting up some swank boutique.

The steamer's tank is filled with water. Allie, holding the hose, is misting a black dress with white polka dots worn by a headless store dummy. They sure know how to get their hands on what they need.

"Is that the latest fashion in dresses?" I say.

She ignores me. It's ugly. The polka dots make my eyes swim. No man would feel proud dating a girl wearing that dress.

"Where's the head?" I say. "Are there other heads? Male heads? Switch and swap?"

She swings the sprayer wetting me. "Hey!"

Both break into hysterical laughter.

‡

Actually I've been trying to come up with a business enterprise of my own but my mind is blank. I could do with the extra cash. Not to mention the boredom here is overwhelming. Walking in every day is like walking chest deep in water. I push through the heavy weight with nothing to accomplish. A glance at the tent, from time to time— the extent of my work day.

I say to Quinn, "The Boss could be dead and how would we even know?"

"There'd be a smell. Once you smell that smell you never forget." He bats the air in front of his face.

"What kind of smell?"

"Sweet and sour taken to the 9th degree. Disgusting all at once. Feckin' stings your eyes and gets in your clothes and never washes out. Never! You have to toss your stuff goodbye."

"Does this place seem darker to you?" I say.

"What do you mean?"

"The lighting. Do the lights seem dimmer?"

He's looking up, craning his neck to see the lights further back. "They look about the same."

I rub my eyes. I can't shake the dimness. This space used to feel over lit.

Later on I mention the lights again. "Maybe the building somehow lowered the wattage to save money."

Quinn says, "It's the atmosphere creating a ruckus in your brain. These feckin' girls with their feckin' customers all the day long. I didn't hire on to work in ladies lingerie."

Again I wonder what's going on with his great love Sheilah. I sensed some tension when he said *ladies lingerie.*

"Quinn, if the Boss is in there, do you think he can hear the conversations and all the racket?"

"That's a good question."

If the Boss can hear our noise, does it cause a reaction in him? Or is it just felt like a hum? Like traffic below when you live in a skyscraper. You hear the horns and garbage trucks waking you up every day; but far, far off. Distant noise. And I'm thinking about the Boss's wife and if she ever thinks about him.

CHAPTER 20

The Employee – Siren Song

On my way in this morning, I pause to scan the Lobby Board for other marketing businesses in this building. It would be nice to stay in the building. I'm comfortable here. I can get my paper. If Rosie's re-opens I can get my coffee. If I want to stop into the old office and say hello to Quinn it would be easy. Marketing is all I know. How to push product. The ear swab is all we have left. It's being massacred. Swallowed up by negative media. Cancel culture has done a number on the swab.

Nothing much of interest on the Lobby Board. Scanning from A to Z there's a disproportionate number of therapists, acupuncturists, yoga studios, chiropractors, nutritionists, healers and herbalists. Your basic agenda-driven industries. It used to be lawyers on the board, and small businesses like insurance agents and dentists. Most of them listed now are women. A few men with first names like Herbert and Charles give a clue to their age and experience level. If I were to go to a therapist, it wouldn't be one of these Mirandas or Gillians or Zaras. I would want a man, first of all. Men and women are not the same despite the feminists still pushing for equal rights. I'm not against equal rights. But I've never met a man and woman in a relationship who think the same. If they did, there would be a lot less divorce. If I do choose a therapist, I would want an older man. One who has been around the block.

Stepping out of the empty elevator, I push open the office door like every day. Only now every day brings more anxiety. The first thing to hit me today is approximately five feet tall— a cardboard cut-out of a shapely blonde wearing a bright pink KN95 and the words: *Mask To Save Your Ass & That Of Your Loved Ones. That*??? Which illiterate girl put this sign together?

"*Those* of your loved ones!" I scream across infinity.

Tanya's new sidekick, Tanka, appears from nowhere. Those two flit in and out like mirror images. She's wearing that same pink KN95 without the shapely blondeness. "You have a problem?" she says.

A problem? She should only know. "Did your parents name you Tanka?" If she even has parents. She moves like a robot and has a robot face. I've seen it when she sneaks the mask off.

"You have some nerve!"

Now Tanya's appeared via their magnetic connection. "What did he do?" Tanya wants to know. "Did he touch you inappropriately?"

Tanka hesitates.

"I never laid a hand on her!"

"Tanka is that true?"

"He was getting close to doing it," says Tanka.

That lying bitch. We've had some ragged-ass women work here but never an outright liar in the area of sexual harassment. Tanka has the appeal of a used sponge. "I would rather fondle a snake," I say.

"Just keep your hands to yourself," says Tanya.

"Oh give me a break!"

As they walk away, Tanya slings an arm across Tanka's shoulders.

"Six feet apart!" I shout.

‡

After dusting myself off from that unpleasant start, I look around to see what new commercial enterprise has sprung up. The tent is still pitched in the same spot. Like one of those tiny pre-fab houses. This one happens to sit on lino flooring and leases monthly for over a thousand bucks per square foot. You'd think the Boss, even in his current mental state, once in a while would get the urge to move the tent a few feet. Or turn it so the flap faced a different direction. You'd think he'd get tired of a southern exposure and move it another way. Not that I've ever seen the flap flapping open. Not one time.

Suddenly I'm struck by a thunderbolt. Suppose we were to call in some artists and have them paint mountains across the entire back wall? It could possibly change things bigly. The Boss might walk out of his tent in the middle of the night, knowing he is safe and alone, then see the mountains and think to himself *I could climb those.* The old Boss was that type of man. *Tell me what you need and we'll figure it out,* the old Boss used to say.

I run my mountains idea by Quinn. He listens intently. "It could make a big difference," he says. "Either he'll kill himself trying to go mountain climbing or he'll wake the hell up and face the facts."

"It can't continue like this."

"Shite. I'm ready to pull up stakes and go back to Ireland for good."

"Really?"

"Well. Unless I come up with something myself on the side."

"Like what?"

He's already got his pub across the pond and god knows what else. The office is shaping up to be a cross between the lobby at Bellevue Hospital, jam packed with street vendor displays, and a wild bazaar in some exotic land. All that's missing is the frenetic music, and the spices and skunk pot soaking the air.

Quinn, drumming his fingers on a desk, looks solemn. Money. Its own siren song.

"OK I'll call in a painter I know," he says heading toward his cubicle.

"Tell him to make it realistic," I yell.

He looks back at me. "Realistic? Don't we have enough of that already?"

"Well, somewhat realistic."

CHAPTER 21

The Employee – Thinly Veiled

Later in the day Tanya appears from out of her plastic drapes with new pink hair. Pink mask, pink hair. "Pretty in pink," I say. My feeble attempt at reconciliation.

"I have to stay au courant."

"What about Tanka, she gone pinko too?"

"Fuck you. See this is why you have no friends." Her stilettos click away toward her scrub hut.

No friends? What a laugh. She should know how tight I was with the Boss. I probably know more about his private life than anyone else here. Not that I know all that much. Who does? The Boss played things close to the vest.

Maybe I should step out and get a Starbucks to go. I'm dragging. It might pick up my energy. I wonder about the Boss alone here at night. Maybe he cavorts through the empty office dancing and singing. Who can say?

I stroll over to the clothes rack area. Stella and Allie have added some fake-antique arm chairs in bright-red cut-velvet, and a tall Chinese vase filled with floppy white feathers that sway in the air flow. "Staying au courant?" I say copying Tanya.

"We want it to be as attractive as possible for our customers," says Allie. "We can't have them sitting in office chairs when we have the fashion show."

"Fashion show? This happens to be an office. Did you forget? What if the Boss wanders out in the middle of your runway gig?" They both look at me stone-faced. "It's a very good idea, don't get me wrong, but not here," I say. "Would you each like a Starbucks?" I'm concerned Allie could grab the steamer and hose me again.

They just ignore me. I thought we three might sit together sipping coffee in their new chairs. It would be a nice change of pace.

Seeing it's pointless, I cross the width of the room in the direction of the tent. I have no idea why. Usually I regard the tent like a mine field in the desert. A blow up that could come at any moment. Not that I expect camels to emerge, and I certainly don't expect to see the Boss. However… I do notice a certain smell; other than the smell of unwashed flesh. Can't quite put my finger on it. While I'm sniffing cautiously, for fear of getting a big stinky blast, DeGrande appears. Mostly these days he's been job ghosting since his lay-off, according to the gossip around here.

"So what are you up to these days?" I say.

He's cagey with those slippery eyes. Something is definitely cooking. Typical DeGrande. Plus he doesn't ask about the Boss, not a word, no *How's the Boss doing.* Nothing. He must still be pissed about the lay-off.

"The least you could do is ask about the Boss."

"Is he still alive in there?"

"Ssshhh! You want him to hear?"

DeGrande laughs his ugly sound that's not a laugh but more of a vocal sneer.

"If you people had half a brain you'd stand here cursing him out all day," says DeGrande. "You'd infuriate him to the point where he'd finally come out and be the Boss again. Instead, you all coddle him. Let him stay in the tent, sulking, or whatever the hell he's doing."

"It is his right to stay in the tent if that's what he wants," I say. "He is the Boss."

"Not if headquarters gets wind of what's going on."

Is DeGrande making a thinly veiled threat? "You don't even work here, anymore," I say.

"When has that mattered where the truth is concerned?"

CHAPTER 22

The Employee – Hot Rage

Kenny has returned, too. Nobody cares. Does he think he can sashay in after all this time and get a hero's welcome?

"I went to talk with the Boss but his office looks pretty much emptied out," Kenny says. "But I see the girls are busy busy busy."

His hair is spiked higher and stiffer. I stare at some point behind him.

"I got tired of working from home," he says. "Will you look at that boutique! Class A. Is that Tanya's set up, too?"

"No."

I find I despise him more than ever.

"And what's with that tent?" he says.

"The tent? Funny you should notice. It's for the customers to put their dogs in while they go through the clothes racks or get their beauty treatments."

Kenny is nodding. "Very sensible."

I scream, "You fucking idjit!!!" so loud he jumps back.

"You can't find the Boss in his office, Kenny, because the Boss is living in the tent! That tent! There!" I stab the air repeatedly with my finger. "And for a while now! You saying one of the others didn't tip you off about the tent? And that's the only reason you came back?"

"I swear I had no idea!"

I can feel the bile rising in my throat. I suddenly realize that I love the Boss. Not in a sexual way, but like a father or older brother. I want to punch Kenny in the nose. "You know what, Kenny, I don't believe you. You're the type who keeps up with things, wants to be sure he's not missing out."

"That's a total misconception on your part," he says.

"Bull shit."

He moves a chair a few inches for no apparent reason. Stares at it, then sits down. "You've changed," he says. "You were always a quiet sort of smart person. Now you seem a little nuts. Have you thought about counselling? There's a whole load of them listed downstairs..."

The Lobby Directory. "I'm warning you, Kenny."

I shift my glance toward the tent hoping the Boss stays put.

I sense that if he takes this moment to come out, of all possible times, with Kenny right here, will somehow become Kenny's golden opportunity.

Fortunately the Boss stays put.

I've suffered. Months stretching to years. I'm still suffering. I want the old days back. The past has become a meme of its own making. I've tried to maintain normalcy. Does such a thing even exist? What is normal in today's world? Expensive jeans and sneakers? Fancy cars? The latest cell phone? For ladies the $10,000 designer hand bag? Is this what all the wars and deaths and misery have brought us to?

Kenny has been talking. "What?" I say.

"I repeat. We should do an intervention with the Boss. He can't stay in there forever. Someone will report him. I'm sure it violates the building code. Have you peeked inside? What's it like in there?"

"Of course I haven't looked inside!!!" It would be a personal violation; like looking in someone's pants.

I realize I've reached that dark place with all kinds of catchy phrases: *Dark night of the soul* being a standard. I've reached hatred. I hate this big empty room so much my body feels emptied out, too. I swear I can hear one bone knocking against the other when I move. A mad dash to escape. Where would my bones go? A tent?

Silent, I walk away from Kenny.

The girls are setting out new merchandise, unpacking boxes, hanging stuff. They ooh and aah and giggle and gab. So much happier than when the focus was ear swabs. Allie holds up a wide red belt with silver studs. "This one's nicked a little, right here, see?"

Stella snaps, "It goes back." They're meticulous. I admire their fastidiousness about their merchandise but I still can't stand them. I hate them all now. To them the Boss doesn't exist.

"I'm going home," I say to no one in particular.

PART THREE

CHAPTER 23

The Employee – Doors

The across-the-hall neighbor tells me he hasn't been back to work in two years. All gets done strictly from his apartment. He's wearing pj's. Sporting a white beard that covers his face sporadically. The pink parts of skin that show through look indecent. I say a few things back to his few things, attempting to act friendly in return. Finally I tell him I have a pile of work to catch up on. We say *See ya! See ya!* Closing our doors. The next time I run into him in the hall by the garbage chute he asks me *What's it like out there?*

"You mean working on the outside?"

"Yeah."

"The same." I scratch my head. Flakes fall. "Pretty much."

He's nodding.

The *Head and Shoulders* isn't working. Stress (the final medi-fomercial I caught) can cause dandruff and seborrhea of the scalp. I'm hoping the neighbor didn't notice the flakes falling past my eyes or maybe stuck to my brows and eyelashes. "Well, the same and different," I add hoping to distract him.

"I may never go back," the neighbor says. "None of those interruptions when you work from home."

"True." I'm not about to go into the peculiarities of my own office situation. "Our building does seems pretty quiet these days," I say. *Our building.* It builds a bond here in case of fire or other mayhem.

The neighbor is on a roll. "I enjoy home life. I have a canary and a cat."

"Isn't that a controversial mix?"

"Dare to be different," he says.

As if crouched in his apartment, in pj's, with a cat waiting to spring on a bird is some badge of cool? It's the bird who's got the courage. Poor bird. That's real stress. Probably shits a brick every time the cat slinks past. I want to say *Next time we meet just keep walking.* But with so many fires breaking out in apartment buildings lately it's best to keep up the phony-friendly neighbor routine.

"Have a nice day," I tell the neighbor. He reciprocates the sentiment and we both smile and shut our doors.

After many years in that huge office space, my own place feels seriously cramped under these 24/7 conditions. It's one thing to have a crash pad of sorts and another to call it home. I should probably look around for a spacious apartment since right now the city is loaded with low priced real estate.

I lie on the couch and turn on the tube. Tomorrow is another day.

CHAPTER 24

The Employee – Deficiencies

Each morning I wake up thinking: *Today I'll look for a new place.* Check the realtor listings and see what's what. It would be nice living close to the park. A momentary sizzle ignites my skin. Like when you first get a woman excited and the clothes come tearing off. I haven't been with a woman that way in quite some time.

My food intake is down. I'm tallish, always had a lanky frame; but I think I've dropped around ten pounds. I used to step on the scale in the Mens Room at the office; every so often. Especially after a week of big eating. Such as when we had the client in town and had to show them a good time. The Palm, Sardis. Those upscale French restaurants with the small portions didn't tickle the clients palates.

And even if I had a scale where would I put it? The bathroom can hardly fit a small waste basket. Sink and toilet so tight they're almost married to the tub. At least I have a window in my bathroom. A window in the bathroom or kitchen is a huge big deal in this city.

On occasion when I brought a woman home, sooner or later they'd ask to use the bathroom. Emerging, every one of them was a bit cuckoo over the window; practically squealing: *A window in a New York apartment bathroom*!!! (in this rent range practically unheard of). When I moved here, I had no idea it would have this kind of affect on women. I always nodded acting humble; like it was me they were nuts over.

On the couch mostly, watching movies, another day passes. This couch for my height is short a good 12 + inches. Forcing me to scrunch up. If I'd been able to snag Stella, this couch would never do. I'd have to buy a sectional so she could spread out her silly self. That style tends to run expensive. Still, it would be worth every cent to see her tits pointing skyward before climbing on top of her. It would be heaven. I'm wondering if the Boss can stretch out in his tent? My phone bleeps a few times but I don't even look.

Steering clear of the news I click the remote toward something less dreary. I don't need dreary. I can do dreary by myself. Before this pandemic I'd hear the world's dreary and it would register a twinge in me. A twinge. Then life would go on. Now my life seems ground down like old wet coffee beans. By choice some would say. My choice. I'm no activist. No plan in the works to chain myself to a parking meter because I have to wear a mask when I go to the movies.

Getting up, stretching, I'm debating whether to have a beer. Wondering if the painted mountains on the back wall have been done? What season the artist painted into the mountains? I really should have been there to control things. No way would I have allowed a winter mountain range. Quinn, being a skier, probably had them paint some replica of The Alps. Goddammit! I visualize something more along the line of mountains in springtime. A few sprouts of green coming up at the base. A few very early blooms in yellow.

The Boss in his night time wanderings— did he even notice mountains in his midst?

I grab a beer, open it, sit on the couch leaning forward. I'm starting to realize certain truths. Such as the tremendous hold the Boss has over my life; even before this damned virus struck. The Boss. He crept up on me. I don't feel it was intentional. He's a boss. It's what bosses do. They seek control. I don't necessarily like this realization. I hate knowing anyone has a hold over me. Probably why I haven't had a lasting romantic relationship. The problem, I realize, is coming from me. And only me. And now I start hating myself.

‡

Taking a sheet of paper from the computer tray I start listing my deficiencies:

Lousy apartment.

Inadequate couch.

No love life.

No pets.

No new clothing for several years.

No gym or personal trainer.

An old Omega watch that needs batteries every few months.

Sparse contact with my one sibling, a sister. (In all fairness she now lives in the hills of Montana which is a bitch to get to. A couple of plane transfers then a long ride on Trailways).

No paint job in this apartment for over a decade.

I'm starting to slow down here. I'm sure I'll come up with more. The kitchen! — could use a serious remodeling or at least cabinet door veneers and a new countertop.

‡

The gel pen I'm using leaked black on the side of my fingers. Placing the list on the chipped countertop, I go back to the couch, lying down, on my other side. This way the cramp from my scrunched leg will be evenly transferred.

CHAPTER 25

The Employee – West Facing

West facing, this apartment is mostly dark. The sun moves behind buildings before this place can absorb any decent amount
of light. This situation was basically unknown to me. Or, at least
ignored. When things are normal, who pays attention to the small
deficiencies. I'm thinking if the virus had never struck, I wouldn't
know I live in a dark apartment. Having to keep the lights lit
during daytime. Otherwise— a dark presence is constantly surrounding me.

The Boss chose to have a dark presence hovering when he
stepped into the tent.

Come Monday morning I shower and shave and get dressed
for work.

CHAPTER 26

The Employee – Mountains

The first thing I see when I step in are mountains — huge and cresting, covering the entire back wall, roughly 80 feet — I rub my eyes. Or is it 800 feet? stretching skyward floor to ceiling. Mountains and more mountains. I'm gaping.

A few of the girls call out tepid *Hellos*. They must've missed me. No scapegoat for them while I was gone. I'm still glued to the floor, lock-jawed. These mountains — beyond my wildest imaginings.

Stella walks over looking me up and down. "Did you have a nice rest?"

"Rest?"

The only strange thing about the mountains is how they navigate the Boss's office door. All glass, it's cut in and off to the side — now in the midst of these soaring peaks. But that hardly matters. Whoever painted these mountains brought life into this desolation.

"Who is the artist?" I ask Stella.

"Tanya found him. She knows everyone who's anyone. They were here photographing the other day. I think it's going to be in The Atlantic. Well one of those hip mags."

"What? Photographing the mountains?" I turn toward the Boss's tent. Gone. I feel a ticking clock working my brain. "Where is the tent?"

"Quinn had them take it down before the photo shoot. He said it made the place look crazy."

The place is crazy. "Was the Boss in there?"

"I don't know," says Stella.

A man she works for, her Boss, and his temporary shelter have gone missing. And yet she knows nothing.

Allie comes over shaking out a garment. "This will have to be steamed before we can rack it," she tells Stella.

"Maybe *you* know where the Boss is?" I say.

"Janice took him home."

Janice? "The wife?"

"The one and only," she says. "I think she plans to take the Boss to a spa."

"What spa? Where?"

"Maybe Iceland? She said it has to be a country with a low case count."

At least that makes a little sense.

"How did the Boss seem?"

"Fine."

Stella nods. "Yeah he was the same only dirtier."

"Did he have the Cheetos orange on his hands?" I say.

"I didn't really notice," says Stella. Allie nods in agreement.

Do either of you have one single thought independent of the other? I flex my weak knee. Too much time on the couch. Trying to stay composed I say, "When is the Boss expected back?"

One shakes her head while the other shrugs. "I guess you could always phone Janice," Stella says. "We have to get our racks ready."

Of course! Silly me. I follow them over to their area.

"Who is the Boss for now?"

"No Boss. We're an independent commune," Allie says.

"But you still get a paycheck off the ear swab, right?"

Both girls nod casually. It's now an expectation. They go on sorting through the clothing, holding certain items against themselves, making comments over this or that one.

Quinn and Kenny stroll over wearing big fake smiles.

CHAPTER 27

The Employee – Cancel

"Hey."

"Hey."

"Hey."

Each waiting for another to blow out the latest dirt.

"So, Janice," I say finally. "She came and picked him up?"

"That's about the size of it," says Kenny.

"Did he put up a struggle?"

Quinn chortles. "Quiet like a lamb to the slaughter."

My empty hand clenches into a fist; I tell myself *relax... relax...* Tossing my backpack with more than the required energy.

"What about DeGrande what's he doing here? The Boss laid him off."

Both men start laughing. Finally Kenny says, "He's got some bubble head product idea for medical."

Medical. Bound to happen. What with the medi-fomercials coming off the widescreen in a constant stream. Impending disaster permeating the air. DeGrande and impending disaster = perfect combo.

"He has no right," I say.

Kenny starts whistling.

‡

Even if you don't pay attention, those medi-fomercials worm their way in. Everyone here knows ear swabs are deader than dead. Three years ago an ENT Doc canceled my appointment after he found out my method for getting out wax (he didn't even know we market the swab). Doc Ear had strolled in to the little room all smiley face then he grilled me. Calling the ear swabs: *Those things on a stick.* Couldn't bring himself to say an actual brand name. Then he told me: *Be right back.* A few minutes later a tech appeared saying *Your appointment has been cancelled.* Three years ago! *Cancel* was already in the works; churning through our pathetic cultural history.

"What exactly is DeGrande's big idea?" I say to Quinn.

"It's all very hush hush. You know how grand DeGrande can

be. He orates rather than dump his load." He's fumbling for his flask taking a swig.

"So what is it?"

"Seems to be a variation on that Q Grip. The one like a corkscrew that twists to catch the wax while you get to watch inside your ear on a little screen."

Wax on a little screen. "Don't tell me anything else," I mutter through a yawn.

"Did time away cheer you up, Mate?"

Cheer me up? What planet does he inhabit? "Too many dead people."

The men are silent. Quinn crosses himself. Kenny looks around rather than confront the issue.

'Cause deep down, death is some far away notion to them. Till someone they know croaks. Same with the girls— keeping it at bay with the pretty clothes they sell. Even for me, on some level. A black cloak with a scythe in the night. Yet the bodies keep piling up. The streets of this city are mourning. Every step, death underfoot.

Now Janice has removed the Boss. Tent or no tent, he was my last bastion of civility. After that baby business flopped she actually left the Boss! Or he left her. The sequence is confusing. I don't trust her; her instincts or her choices. The whole spa thing sounds fishy.

"Those mountains are inspiring." I walk away from Quinn and Kenny to get a closer look.

The muted greens and blues and a reddish-brown color appear brighter the closer I get. These are some beautiful mountains. I pull a chair over and sit down facing the back wall. The painter managed some very blue sky and a bright glaze over the scene. I could almost pitch a tent, myself, beside these mountains. I think it could make me happy again. Maybe that's what the Boss thought when he entered his tent.

My reverie is short lived. "You came back to us, after all."

Tanya. Sure can take the bloom off the bud. Or, the rose off the thorn? I don't know. I don't know all the little things I used to know by heart.

"Hello." A new dull tone to my voice.

"You heard about the Boss, I presume?"

"Uh huh."

"What do you think?"

"About what?"

She's stalling. What's on her beady little mind?

"I was wondering if the whole place will come down now that the Boss is gone."

Self-interest. What a surprise.

"I wouldn't know." I refuse to make eye contact, staying focused on the mountains. Though I did notice her hair is Kelly Green. Hard to miss that. I swallow. Leaves a wintergreen air freshener taste stuck in your throat.

"If the company is going to vacate I'd like some advance notice," she says. "For my customers. Plus, I'll need time to find another place to set up shop."

What's she telling me for? I don't give a shit about her shop. "I suppose you will," I say.

Not a single word out of her about the Boss. As if the Boss never hired her, let her put the damn beauty spot in that corner, and was a generally good guy to everyone. All but forgotten now. The tent has come down. Last remnants of the Boss. Someone should be playing TAPS.

"Are you planning on setting up a little enterprise of your own?" Tanya continues along this line, bending at the waist to try and engage me through eye contact.

"As a matter of fact, yes! Those chambers where you freeze people."

"I don't find that especially funny."

"Just think, when they de-freeze all this will be over. And meantime you won't need a dye job for ages."

That got rid of her. Though I didn't watch, I felt her scamper despite her stiletto heels.

CHAPTER 28

The Employee – Lifelike Yet Surreal

At least there's *something* in this huge space to feast your eyes on. So lifelike yet surreal. The way we live. I used to spin my old high school globe then put my finger on a country and think *I could live there.* Or, *there.* No longer. I'm rooted here. Others seem more adaptable. What does that say?

Green grassy wisps painted near the lower base with little splashes of the red-brown, some yellow flower wisps coming up, and the cold white tips toward the very top peaks with a fresh blue sky hovering— perfection. As if the painter read my mind. I'm feeling overwhelmed but choke it back. "Where is the god-damn tent?" I yell at the top of my lungs.

Tanya or is it Tanka (both sporting the green hair) pokes a head out of the plastic. "Please! You're disturbing the serenity in here."

"Which one are you?"

"I'm Tanka, jerk."

"All right. Do you happen to know where the tent is stored? Tanka?"

She frowns making it clear I have really annoyed her. "In the Boss's office." She disappears behind the plastic.

Well that was easy. The first easy thing in— like a long time. I take a deep breath. I need to inspect that tent. See what clues I can gather about the Boss and his living conditions. "Does any-one have a magnifying glass?" I yell.

Since the tent has been moved, and the contents are gone, I will need to make an extremely close inspection for fluids, fibers, food particles; that sort of thing.

"A magnifying glass!" I scream again.

Tanka comes through the plastic. "This is all we've got!" Thrusting a round pink mirror at me. "One side is magnified."

I take it by the long plastic handle. "This is useless."

"Get lost," she says, attempting to grab it back.

I hold it out of reach and we have this sort of untouched tussle till she gives up, curses, and goes back through the plastic. I watch to see if she'll return with some type of weapon. When things on that front appear quiet, I slowly approach the Boss's office with trepidation. As if he might be living there; in his altered state. Possibly in attack mode. Not remembering who I am. I picture the Boss as a huge bear. Hungry from his hibernation and scarce food intake consisting mainly of Cheetos.

His door is locked. Not stuck, but definitely locked. What the fuck! This only confirms my suspicions. There was no Janice pick up. The Boss is hiding out in his office. Then I notice his door knob has an outer key lock, too. Someone else might have an extra key. The Boss never locked his office. Either he's locked in or he's locked out. It's all very disturbing.

I stride through the long office space shouting: "Who has the key to the Boss's office!"

Finally Quinn comes forward. "Sorry, Mate. I should have told you."

"You got the damn key?"

"Don't get your knickers in a twist, I got it, it's right here." He smacks his pocket.

"Give it to me." He hands it over with a big smile. I don't thank him.

Back at the Boss's office I try the key and the door opens. I don't step in but reach inside with my arm feeling around the wall for the switch. Bingo! The whole place lights up. I walk in. No Boss. Or anyone else.

But there's the tent. One and the same. The Boss's old habitat mounded sloppily on the floor like it got shoved there in a hurry.

I approach with caution. Not that I expect the Boss to be under there. More concerned it may be harboring a rat or two. This is, after all, a major city. Rats, mice, roaches, bed bugs and other vermin out number people by many, many zillions. This tent, under its folds, must smell of the Boss— his rank unwashed body, his food supply (whatever that was)— all make for a perfect rodent nest.

A new sadness fills me. A good man like the Boss. Such humiliations. These bums working here selling an international news story with pictures!!! And obviously getting a big cash return off the Boss— his trials and tribulations. It's almost too much to take. When the story runs— I shudder— they'll make him out to be a clown, an object of ridicule, or worse— insane. He'll become the subject of cartoons, memes; all the shit that makes people happy these days.

CHAPTER 29

The Employee – History

Not my idea of *good* when Kenny appears in the Boss's office to tell me they're going to have those climbing step / grab things installed on the wall so people can climb the mountains. He rubs his palms together. "It will be great for exercise and morale, dontcha think?"

I'd been staring at the tent which he doesn't even mention. "Great! It'll be great for a lawsuit when someone falls and cracks their skull. Or even dies! You want that on your plate?" (He doesn't have a conscience). "We're not a fitness center."

"Not yet," says Kenny before calling me a downer.

I'm starting to see the ugly picture clearer. Uglier than the belly button worms. "What was your rake-off on the story?"

He lowers his head and slinks away. I tell myself *calm down*.

Then I start the procedure. I start by lifting one fold of the tent. Just one. Slowly. Purposefully. It's a process. In case anything hidden falls loose I don't want to miss it. Also, should something disgusting come running out I want to be able to jump away. Mainly, though, I'm doing it slowly because I don't want to bypass a single thing from the Boss's time in the tent. There is significant history here (not the puffed-up sensationalism some magazine is going to print with photos).

Quinn comes nosing but I send him away.

"There is history here." My voice echoes, which I know has to be impossible. History tattooed on a man's heart.

‡

The tent folds are heavy and cumbersome; a worse jumbled mess than I suspected. The correct way would be to spread out the entire tent on the floor. But the Boss's office isn't big enough. If I drag the whole thing out the door, bits and pieces of his tent life will dislodge and disperse. People will walk over to see what's what and possibly crush important clues. Potentially never to be uncovered.

Hoping like hell for no rodents, I scoop up the tent which is far from easy. Then I can't get out. I'm clutching it trying to get the door to stay open but there's no auto gadget. I'll have to let go of the tent, wedge a chair against the door. Cursing, I drop it and wedge the door open. Sweating. It's winter and I'm sweating. I'll have to start over again carrying the tent out.

Floor junk will taint evidence. I'm careful to look ahead at the floor. If one of those girls or their customers were eating a donut, for instance, some powdered sugar could have dropped to the floor back here or even sprinkles. I'm pretty sure the Boss doesn't eat donuts. But I'm sure he did devour all those Cheetos.

When I've got the tent all spread out on what looks to me like clear floor Quinn returns. "Just checking."

"Not now, I don't want to be distracted."

"You're the boss," he says.

"I – Am – Not – The – Boss!!!!!"

"Easy does it, Mate." He leaves; though not before whistling the Looney Tunes song.

‡

I decide to start by lifting each section after I've examined the outer camouflage part. "It's a process," I repeat. Starting to feel a little nuts myself. Have I taken on more than I can chew? To do this right, I have to first brush down then off— to see if anything drops to the floor. Or falls on my hands. Maybe some food residue; something. Carefully working my way around I brush it with my hands: repeating, repeating, repeating, repeating. Not a bit of anything falls off the tent. So far it seems squeaky clean.

Tanka saunters by hissing "Lieutenant Columbo" at me.

"Stay back!" I warn her.

Once I'm certain the tent's outer portion is clear, I begin by turning it over, section by section; examining the floor under each. Doing the whole interior this way is a bitch. I almost miss a small shred blending into the dirty white floor; almost dismissing it as a thread. Unbelievable! In the palm of my hand sits the remains of a clipped toenail shaped like a half moon. I sit back on my heels studying it.

A man lived in a tent and there is nothing more than this piece of toenail to solidify that existence.

I'm exhausted. It was a big job. I'm feeling parched. A toenail. Not so much as a Tootsie Roll wrapper. The Boss has a fondness for Tootsie Rolls and always kept them in his pocket. Not that he shared. At least not with me. That doesn't matter now. I need information. The Boss lived under this tent 24/7 and I've come up with a partial toenail.

Quinn returns. "Find anything significant?"

I close it in my hand like a stolen diamond. "I haven't found shit."

He chuckles. "You did your best, Mate."

"Yeah."

After my stay at home time I've come to find him somewhat annoying. Not that he's doing anything different. It's my own take on things that's changed. For one thing— I will never do another punchbowl bash. Even on St. Paddy's Day.

Quinn is saying, "The Boss was a devious sort. May have eaten the food wrappings, too. I heard that in wars..."

"Can it, will ya Quinn?"

He raises both hands. "Touchy!"

"Yeah! So now you people are gonna climb the wall? Have you all flipped your cork?"

My outburst doesn't faze him. "You going out for lunch?" he says.

This stupid conversation. Day after day. To lunch or not to lunch. I had a certain life, a way of doing things. Everything's up in the air now.

"I never go out for lunch. You know that. For two plus years I sit in one of the empty cubicles eating a sandwich from home and drinking a Snapple."

"Any special flavor?"

"Piss."

He belly laughs his *ho-ho-ho.* "I had no idea you could be such a prick. It's refreshing."

"You've learned something new."

"What did you learn?" says Kenny walking over lighting a cigarette.

"He learned I'm a prick."

"I knew that," says Kenny. "The quiet ones are always pricks. They hold the venom in. The loud mouths don't have the stuff to be a prick. They let it all out and suffer the consequences."

"Since when did smoking indoors become legal again in New York City?" I say.

CHAPTER 30

The Employee – Heel

I slip the toenail clipping into my pocket. "Can you help me drag the tent back in the Boss's office?"

"Normally I wouldn't," Quinn says. "But being that you've admitted you're a prick, and you've already done the hard part... in that case I'll help."

"I'll lend a hand," Kenny says. He starts singing 3 Blind Pricks to the tune of Three Blind Mice.

We manage to drag it in leaving a messy pile. No point trying to re-fold. I'm the last to leave. I look around the office taking in the Boss's few things: two pictures, some generic mementos on the shelves. A fake green plant. I guess he didn't want to take the time to water.

Then I pick up his solid gold ear swab encased in plexiglass—a little tomb. Presented to him by headquarters at some special banquet when ear swabs were still at the forefront of medical hygiene. The Boss took great pride in that little gold swab. I once saw him holding it up to the ceiling lights, turning the cube this way and that. I place it back where it was and switch off the light.

I should choose a cubicle and have my lunch but my damn appetite has deserted me, too.

‡

When I ring the Boss's doorbell (well his and Janice's) I don't have a clue what to expect. I'm like someone soliciting without their printed material. Janice cracks the door. "Yes?" Her hazel-green eyes are smoldering.

"I came to see the Boss."

"His favorite lackey. He asked, you answered. But, camouflage?" This woman laughs but it's all sarcasm. "Couldn't you have got him basic beige?"

"I had nothing to do with that tent. I swear to you. May I call you Janice?" Before she can answer, "I swear to you, Janice" tumbles out. I hear myself: blurry, foggy, confused.

She opens the door wider. "Come in." Not all that friendly.

I step in cautiously when a large reddish hound makes a beeline for me. Janice says, "Heel, Melvin!" He doesn't. "I said heel! Heel!" He laps my hand with his long tongue. Don't they feed this mongrel? Then I think of the Boss and how the Cheetos sustained him. At least we assume they did.

Finally I manage to shove my hand in my jacket. "I didn't realize the Boss had a dog. And, you, as well," I add. Did that sound like I'm saying she is also a dog? Nothing is coming out right.

"Sit down." Commando style; like it's Melvin she's ordering around.

"Here?" A big plush burgundy colored couch with off-white leather toss pillows is the focal point of their living room. The apartment being of those classic pre-wars, Upper East side. I can see a long hallway that probably leads to several bedrooms and even an extra bathroom.

"Yeah, there," she says. Looking me over, top to bottom, slowly, an interrogator getting ready to torture.

Then, nothing. Melvin retreats in the silence. This large living room makes silence different than the silence of my own (small) living room. I cough a few times to be sure this is all real.

"Would you care for some juice?"

"Juice?" I put down my backpack and sit where she indicated. The office has been flooded with juice since they ordered that goddamn juicer. I'm aware of my rapid eye movements. Who knows— Janice could tamper with the juice; it may be a ruse; anything's possible. She despising me at this level. "I don't think so," I say.

"What can I do for you?" She doesn't sit down.

"For me? Nothing really." The rug is one of those Oriental carpets that looks expensive. I wonder if the Boss walks barefoot on this rug. "I was sort of hoping to talk to the Boss."

"That's impossible." She's looming now, sort of bent like an arc lamp, still scrutinizing me. Melvin, at least, seems down for the count, drowsing near a radiator under the picture window. It draws a lot of light into the room. Not like the tent. In the quiet, I listen. No sound of the Boss. That doesn't mean he's not here. We never heard a sound coming from the tent.

"Can you at least tell me where he might be at the moment?"

"My husband needs total serenity. His body is full of scabs. Did you know that?" I shake my head that I didn't. "Even his scalp," she goes on. "I can't get him to stop picking. It's terrible. As soon as he picks one off another scab forms in its place."

"I think scabs are supposed to be good," I tell her. "They're part of the natural healing process."

"Not if you keep picking over and over and they never heal!"

I'm nodding and nodding as Janice goes on about the scabs; how it's a serious psychological disorder, that basically the person is trying to pick off all the skin from their body. "Now why would that be?" she says.

"Sorry, but I have no idea."

"I will tell you why. Once you pick all your skin off you no longer resemble the human race."

Wow.

It does kind of make sense. In a crazy sort of way. He did live in a tent and exhibited animal-type behavior when he finally came out.

"Maybe if I talked to him, maybe I could convince him to leave the scabs alone."

I don't think she even heard that.

"My husband doesn't need any reminders of the office." She continues to loom spreading her misery. That damn *dark night of the soul* thing is percolating in my mind again.

"I may be leaving the office," I say. Hoping by disassociating with the office she might see me in a new light.

"That means you and the rest of them," she says like I never said what I said. "And ear swabs, and constant pressure from the company. Pressure that's gone on far too long. Is it his fault that our violent culture has vilified a stick with cotton ends?"

I switch my position on the couch. The softness is too cushy to offer any real back support. Plus my one knee that's been bothersome is starting up. "Oh, I know. It's ridiculous. They don't mind people vaping which is reportedly very bad on the lungs, but use a simple ear swab..."

A recent medi-fomercial showed photos of the lung damage being done by vaping. The girls had watched raptly. Tanka taking notes on her phone which I found a tad overkill.

Janice, meanwhile, has turned away and seems to be talking to herself, walking in circles on a carpet which I'm sure will outlast her. Doesn't she know how many hours of slave labor it takes to weave one of these carpets? I'm hoping her pacing doesn't agitate Melvin to action.

"When he found out there was lobbying in Washington against the swab it nearly broke him! Lobbying!" She stops to look at me. Her eyes bulging. "Those people will do anything to appease the deep pockets. The evil swab! Began to trend on social media. Then a meme, and other memes." She stops to catch her breath. "It was the final straw."

The final straw. The one that broke the camel's back. *Her.*

No wonder the Boss resorted to a tent. Plus this couch sucks. And as for Janice...

"Look, I want you to know that honestly, honestly, I had nothing to do with the tent. I was as surprised as you were." Though I'm wondering why he didn't book a simple hotel room?

She puts her hands over her ears and shuts her eyes. "It's been pressure to the point where my head feels clogged. Like my ear drums are about to burst."

Ear drums. Even Janice has become indoctrinated.

"And I don't even work in that place," she says.

But, do you still use the swab?

It's hopeless. I stand up. Melvin stays settled having a grumbly dog dream.

CHAPTER 31

The Employee – One & the Same

Ghosting jobs, ghosting friends and relatives. Anything with a beating pulse. These streets are ghost streets. They used to be tough to navigate with so many residents and tourists and the work force out and about. Except for a short spell living on the west coast, I've been in this city most of my life.

As I move down 75th Street, away from the Boss's apartment, the sidewalk narrows from scaffolding. Nobody can agree on the virus protocols yet they always agree on scaffolding. Take The French Building on Fifth Avenue. Scaffolded almost a decade. Ten years of not being able to see that incredible vintage façade dripping its gold trim. I used to go to a dentist in there. Just about the time I stopped seeing him due to his carelessness with sanitary habits, they finally took down the scaffolding. The French Building shone. I used to cross Fifth in order to stare over and take in its full glory. Now I have no reason to enter The French Building. May never have a reason the rest of my life. Maybe the Boss will feel the same, now that the tent is dismantled. He might sneak back some night for a secret sleep-over, finding it gone and thinking: No reason to enter, ever again.

When I get back to the office Quinn and his golden retriever have center stage. At least this dog ignores me. Apparently Quinn put the dog through a rigorous training program and now he's showing the results. The dog can dance on his two hind legs like a circus elephant act. After each little dance Quinn rewards the dog with a biscuit. I can't remember the dog's name. Everyone claps. If the Boss ever comes back will people clap?

"Mate, what do you think?" Quinn calls out to me.

"Yeah, terrific."

He squints. "Something the matter?"

I cock my head slightly to indicate he should meet me in the rear. His eyes indicate he's aware. I start toward the mountains.

"We'll do it one more time and call it quits," Quinn tells his small audience.

Meanwhile, DeGrande is trailing me calling out, "Wait up!"

The last person I want to deal with. I feel him closer practically feel his breath on my neck. I stop walking without turning around.

"What do you think of Mt. Rushmore?" says DeGrande.

According to him, the girls have named the mountains Rushmore. It fits. The world, everything in it, rushing frantically toward nothingness. Rushmore in this office space is both an inspiration and harbinger of doom. DeGrande pokes me on the shoulder.

"What is it?" I'm actually talking to the beautiful mountains. I can't turn around and look at that half-baked pancake.

"You have to promise to keep this to yourself," he says.

"Keep what?"

"I'm serious, man. Word cannot get out."

He steps in front of me so now I'm forced to look at him.

"Why tell me if it's so top secret?" Why tell anyone?

"I trust you. Instinct," he says.

The backpack is weighing on my shoulder. What do I even need it for? Protection? There is no protection. My energy sucks lately, I can carry my lunch in a paper bag. DeGrande seems to be waiting for me to say something back. I want to say *I'm not your new best friend*. This is the guy who had an instinct about ear swabs and icing.

"What is it?" I don't care if there's hostility in my tone.

"You know Janice, right? The Boss's wife?"

Did he follow me there?

The backpack slides down my arm to the floor. Or maybe he had me followed. Is this about extortion? He's dumb but I sense him easily capable of great harm. I've always doubted his name. DeGrande. Sounds too made up and theatrical.

I clear my throat several times. "So what about the Boss's wife?"

"She's pregnant."

How the hell would DeGrande know something this personal?

I'm staring over his shoulder at Rushmore, trying to piece it together; buying time. Like I've been doing ever since the virus hit. Or as Quinn calls it: *Tap dancing in place*.

"That's nice she finally got pregnant," I say. "Those are some fucking beautiful mountains."

DeGrande actually moves to block my view. An odd look on his odd face. Unusually flushed. A red pancake. I almost crack up laughing, expecting little air holes to pop. *Time to flip the pancake,*

Mom would say. I miss my family. The ones I haven't seen for so long. The ones who are dead. And I miss the Boss. His comforting presence. I miss just about everything that may never be whole again like Humpty Dumpty when he fell off the wall.

"It's not his," DeGrande says.

Did I just step out of a cryogenic chamber? Has the world moved on while I waited out better times in the deep freeze? My mind is spinning. The Boss despises him— he would never confide in this guy. DeGrande is playing some angle here, trying to reel me in. The little fish. That's how he sees me. I knew it from the beginning.

"What's your game, DeGrande?"

"It's mine," he says.

A power play for the Boss's office? Again! He wants me on his side against the rest of them.

"You can't take over the Boss's office just because he's not using it at the moment."

"Not the office." His voice sounding rough and gravely. "The baby."

All of a sudden I'm extremely cold. My face, my hands and feet. Like I'm outside and the wind is tearing through Times Square so hard and fast it's almost a solid.

"I don't believe you."

"It's true," he says.

"How do you know?"

"Because the Boss has been in the tent all this time."

DeGrande. A worse asshole than I ever suspected. "Maybe she's been screwing other guys, too. How do you know you're the one?"

"She said it's mine."

"Janice?"

He's looks calmer now that he let out his secret. Even his face is back to its regular pancake color.

"Now I get why you thought you could make an ear swab into a cake decorating tool. You're dumb, dumber than shit to do the deed with her. Not to mention mean. You're a mean sucker, DeGrande. Here was the Boss rotting under our noses. And you over at the pre-war fucking his wife."

"It's gotta be worth 2 mil."

"You bum."

I'm wondering if he'll move in once the baby is born.

"Every night?" I can't help asking.

"Days. Mostly."

It doesn't mean she couldn't have other guys on the off times. Janice was desperate. Maybe she figured she couldn't have too many sticks in the fire.

A hideous sounding laugh blasts out of me like an unsuspecting fart; from a dark and rotting place. What Quinn called *the dark environs*. I'm not shocked. I knew I was rotting away. But DeGrande looks shocked and more than a little worried.

"Which one of you is going to break this to the Boss?" I say.

Break his heart being more to the point.

CHAPTER 32

The Employee – Life Goes On

The widescreen has been removed. Something about a donation. The beauty spot, the clothing racks and fancy red chairs and accessory items— history. Tanya, I heard, tried to wrangle a position in the company for Tanka, to no avail. Stella and Allie begged to at least be able to keep the long white feathers and the big vase. No go. The mini-fridge under the reception area is empty of Cheetos. And all other edibles. The juicer sits on the counter washed and covered with a brown paper towel from the bathroom. Rest in peace.

The girls had plenty to say but the Boss turned a deaf ear.

Today the Boss is extolling the greatness of our new marketing product: CLEOPATRA. A unique battery-operated foot sander with automatic moisture cream dispenser attached. He wants our creative input.

"Many people still won't risk getting a pedicure during these uncertain times," he's saying. "CLEOPATRA will sand away the callouses and rejuvenate their feet with creamy moisture. I want ideas, people, ideas!"

The Boss. In very top form: Midnight-blue glove-leather Armani fitted jacket, dark-gray Armani T, straight jeans. Pricey Italian sneakers. How do I know it's Armani? When I complimented him, he told me: *All Armani.* That's the Boss— no beating around the bush, no pretense. No lying and saying the GAP. He's the Boss and he's all Armani.

Another silver frame has been added to his desk. Janice snuggling their new baby. A boy they named Jake.

"All ideas, concepts, etc etc etc will be signed off by me and only me!" says the Boss. He's energized. "Got it?" There are murmurs and nods. "No more crap like that cake decorating screw up."

On *screw* I flinch. DeGrande is bye bye. I don't know the details and don't want to know. He disappeared during the pregnancy. Quinn said he heard the Boss tell DeGrande *Never darken our doorstep.* Which got me to thinking: Did the Boss mean the office doorstep, or the one to his own spacious pre-war apartment which I suspect is a *Classic 5*; in New York real estate lingo.

A riddle not to be solved.

The Boss has never been more on top. He's developed this even stronger inner force. Let's face it— living in a tent in the middle of your workplace, in mid-town, definitely requires fortitude. When Janice brings the baby to the office, on occasion, covertly I examine the little round face. Bubbly with bright cheeks. No sign of DeGrande's pancake on this kid. Quinn calls him a *wee lad*. Time will tell if Jake grows up resembling the Boss. It doesn't really matter. Janice seems softer. Her hair looks good cut and styled in long, casual waves. The Boss is happy because she's happy. The office has better juju. Everything that happened seems like a long bizarre dream. The Boss has let the mountains stay (for the time being). He says he admires their subliminal product message: *Climb hard and go high.*

The Boss did make one new rule on dress code: No camouflage.

As time goes on, the Boss speaks less and less about the swab. Personally, I think it was his favorite product of all time. Why? Because it became so damned impossible. And the Boss is built for challenge. Now more than ever. Once I heard him talking about the days when Kings and Queens had the tiniest miniature solid gold spoons to dig out ear wax. He was practically rhapsodic.

Eventually, after being gently prodded on the whys and wherefores of taking up residence in the tent, the Boss kept it simple: *Because I could.*

Susan Isla Tepper

Susan Isla Tepper has been a writer for twenty years and is the author of ten published books of fiction and poetry and two stage plays. She writes in all genres, with stories, poems, interviews, essays and opinion columns published worldwide. An award-winning author, Tepper received a Pulitzer Prize Nomination for the novel 'What May Have Been' (adapted for the stage and re-titled The Crooked Heart, it is currently in production). She was a winner in the Francis Ford Coppola Zoetrope Contest for the Novel (2003), Second Place Winner in Story/South Million Writers Award, winner of Best Story of 17 Years of Vestal Review, received 19 Pushcart Prize Nominations and several for Best of the Net. Her suspense story 'Africa... then' (in Gargoyle Magazine) was nominated for Best American Thriller/Suspense Series.

Many of her works have been performed onstage. 'Deer' the title story of her collection DEER & Other Stories (Wilderness House Press, 2009) was performed at Inter/Act Theatre in Philadelphia, and at NPR's Selected Shorts.

For seven years Tepper was a panel moderator at the annual Hunter College Writer's Conference.

She created then curated 'FIZZ' a popular reading series at KGB Bar, NYC, which ran for a decade and showcased the talents of our literary stars as well as many first time authors.

Additionally, Tepper was co-editor of the Istanbul Literary Review until it ceased publication several years ago due to political turmoil in that country.

Before settling down to the writing life, Susan Isla Tepper was an actress, singer, flight attendant, interior decorator, TV Producer, rescue worker and more. She blames it all on a high interest range. Tepper is a native New Yorker..